SECRETS UNDERCOVER

A Collection of Poetry and Short Stories from Writers of the Franklin County Library System

SECRETS UNDERCOVER

A Collection of Poetry and Short Stories from Writers of the
Franklin County Library System

Caffeinated Fiction Publishing
Mont Alto, Pennsylvania

Original Copyright ©2025 by Franklin County Library System of Pennsylvania
Visit our website at www.discovery.fclspa.org

All rights reserved.

No part of this publication may be reproduced, distributed, or transmitted in any form or by any means, including photocopying, recording, or other electronic or mechanical methods, without the prior written permission of the publisher, except as permitted by U.S. copyright law. For permission requisitions, contact authors through the Franklin County Library System, Chambersburg, Pennsylvania.

All stories, all names, characters, and incidents portrayed in this production are fictitious. No identification with actual persons (living or deceased), places, buildings, and products is intended or should be inferred.

NO AI TRAINING: Without in any way limiting the authors' exclusive rights under copyright, any use of this publication to "train" generative artificial intelligence (AI) technologies to generate text is expressly prohibited. The authors reserve all rights to license uses of this work for generative AI training and development of machine learning language models.

Published by Caffeinated Fiction Publishing
Mont Alto, PA 17237

FIRST EDITION: 2025

Printed in the United States of America

ISBN-13: 9798991495844

Fiction: Literature and Fiction
Fiction: Collections and Anthologies
Fiction: Short Stories and Poetry

Cover Image by James P. Barkley

Cover Design by Laura L. Zimmerman

❀ Formatted with Vellum

Dedication

*For **Eric D. Bell**, a beloved member of the Quill and Ink Society since its inception. His poems inspired and encouraged the group, and echoed unity, peace, and equality, even after death. His passion to see change in the world will be truly missed. May his spirit and deep faith continue to shine in us all.*

TABLE OF CONTENTS

POETRY

FANTASY + SCI-FI

GENERAL FICTION

BLUE LINES, RED MARKS

by Carol Kagan

*Rosamond Lucille (Harris) Moore, 83, of Mayville,
Pennsylvania, passed away peacefully at home
surrounded by family and friends on August 19, 2011.*

*Rose is survived by her daughter, Cynthia and son-in-
law, Jeffery Masters; daughter, Ella and son-in-law,
Daniel Mott; Grandchildren Holly and Susan
Masters and Douglas and Laurel Mott; sister Karen
(Harris) and husband, George Brown; and many
loving friends. She was preceded in death by her
Husband, Neil.*

*Rose was born on May 1, 1928, in Mayville, was a 1944
graduate of Mayville High School, and a 1948 grad-
uate of Slippery Rock University with a Bachelor of
Arts degree. She was active in Icehouse Playhouse
productions, volunteered at the Wilmington Library,
and loved to travel with family and friends.*

Their mother's attic was dusty, and Cindy and Ella kept
sneezing. Ella's handkerchief hid the tears that came each time

she opened a box or drawer. Even an old handbag, when unclasped, had the powdery scent of her mother's perfume. When they were young, the sisters went to Kaplan's Department Store to buy her a birthday gift. The deep blue bottle of Evening in Paris, with the shiny silver cap, was beautiful and perfectly priced. Their mother loved it and every birthday and Christmas thereafter a new bottle arrived. It became her signature scent.

A warm, woody aroma rose up as Cindy opened the old cedar chest. She was expecting linens and quilts but instead there were black and white composition notebooks, each with a number and letter on the front. Quickly fanning the pages of #1-A, she saw handwritten blue text describing various places and people. Along the margins and intermingled among the words were notes written in red ink adding more thoughts.

"Here's a bunch of Mom's diaries. Do you want to keep them or throw them away?"

Ella looked in the chest. "There certainly are a lot of them. I'm sure there are some sweet memories of family times. She always wanted to be a writer, but it never happened."

"I remember she took a few creative writing classes in college. Some of the writing might be in the diaries," Cindy added.

"If you don't want the cedar chest, just tag it and I'll take it home with the diaries. I'll go through them some day."

Back at home, after days of unloading boxes and furniture including the cedar chest, Ella decided to take a break and read a few diaries. Pulling out the one labeled #1-A, she settled into the recliner with it on her lap and Earl Grey tea with gingersnaps on the side table.

It was filled with blue lines of text and there were red marks with notes along the page edges and others floating over red carets poking into sentences here and there. The heading at the top was *The Purse*. She didn't remember anything in particular that happened in the family with a purse but started reading.

By the time she got to page three she realized this wasn't a diary entry, it was a story, maybe written for school. The main character, Cynthia Miller, found a purse, elaborately decorated, with a secret message inside. Cynthia was curious and began investigating the mysterious message. Ella enjoyed this story and kept on reading to book #1-D. It was well-written but didn't seem to be the full story. During the rest of the week, she read a few more, all handwritten in blue ink with corrections and additions marked in red ink. Each numbered set was a different story.

After a few weeks off, Ella was looking forward to getting back to work at the library. Ann Sylvester, library assistant, was at the checkout desk and greeted her with a hug.

Holding her at arm's length Ann said, "Welcome back." Then quietly asked, "How are you doing?"

"It's good to be here," Ella replied while stashing her bag in a drawer. "The house is for sale and I'm back home now. I'm also ready to work. What needs to be done this morning?"

"There are several carts full of fiction books from weekend returns. They are ready to go back on the shelves."

"That's good. I like reshelving and looking at the returned books. It helps to know what people are reading and gives me some ideas for books to suggest."

After putting the books in author-alphabetical order, she picked each out, looked at the inside cover to read the overview of the story, found its spot on the shelf and slipped it in.

When she got to *The Secret Inside* by Lucy Thompson, she noticed the cover photo of a purse decorated with red flowers and blue beading. The inside description was

*The Old Mill Players were staging **"The Mystery of Miz Arnette"** performance. It's set in Oklahoma during the 1934 Dust Bowl and involves a mysterious woman who rents a room from a desperate farm family. Cynthia Miller, in search of costumes and stage props for the show, discovers an unusual*

handbag in a thrift store. It had intricate embroidery and a colorful peacock with flowing silver sequin feathers and eye-catching red crest and head on the front, perfect for Miz Arnette. Opening the handbag, Cynthia breathes in a faint scent of perfume and finds a small envelope with a message that is a mystery all its own.

It was like the purse story in her mother's notebooks.

Ella sat in a nearby chair and while looking through the pages she recognized parts of the story that were the same as in the notebooks. Could her mother have transcribed a handwritten manuscript of Lucy Thompson's? Maybe someone she knew? Why didn't she tell anyone? Why would she keep that secret?

Looking for another Thompson book she found *Beneath the Flowers* where the overview sounded much like *The Buried Box* story in the notebooks. She was determined to compare the edited notebooks to the published books and checked them out.

At home, Ella sat cross-legged on the den floor, the notebook with *The Purse* was open to page one showing the blue lines of text and red marks. She pulled the hardback book onto her lap and began to compare the start of the stories.

The beginning paragraphs of *The Secret Inside* were different than in the notebook, but she found them on page three. The text was the same, word-by-word, with the red marked comments merged into it. The description of the purse on page twenty in the book also matched with the notebook. She continued choosing pages with specific references and descriptions in the book and, when compared to the notebooks, found the same thing to be true. The beginning of *The Secret Inside* was very much like *The Buried Box*.

Ella was pulling out notebooks looking for *The Buried Box* story when she discovered file folders at the bottom of the chest under the piles of notebooks. She spent the rest of the day reading letters, printouts of e-mails, and other papers.

It had been two months since Rose Moore died and her lawyer, Eric King, scheduled an appointment with the family to read her Will. Ella invited the whole family to gather at the empty house known to the family as Grandma Rose's. The invitation included a request to bring a potluck lunch contribution.

It was a cold November day and there was no heat in the house. When Cindy and Jeffrey arrived, he found newspapers and wood for the living room fireplace. Family members arrived carrying boxes, bags, plates, and containers of food along with a variety of paper and plastic items. The cold wind blew in when someone opened the front door and there was grumbling about the weather.

Greetings of "how was the trip," and "what did you bring" were exchanged as everyone fell into a rhythm of setting the table, moving food from one place to another, moving chairs, and negotiating who sits where.

Pulling the lid off a crockpot, Karen asked, "What's in here?"

"It's spiced cider."

"*Spiked* cider?"

"*Spiced* cider, Aunt Karen. We'll be driving over to the lawyer's office later."

When they were all seated, Jeffrey volunteered to say a brief prayer before the meal and, as they had always done at Grandma Rose's house, they reached out to hold hands.

Among the store-bought food of cold-cut hoagies, bags of chips, and fruit salad there was homemade Grandma Rose's cole slaw and Grandpa Neil's corn and tomato salad. The conversation around the table was mostly fond memories. At the end of the meal, Doug brought out a plate, pulled off a foil cover with a flourish, and started handing out cookies.

"I made my infamous Snow on the Mountain chocolate mint cookies. It's been years since I made them for the school holiday greens sale," he said as cookies were passed around.

Before chairs were pushed back and clean-up began, Ella asked, "Would you please stay for a few minutes before we leave?

As some of you may remember, I took Mom's diaries home. Each of you asked me about them at one time or another. I read some of them and want to share a bit with you."

The smell of the dying fire mingled with deep aroma of the last of the apple cider. A tin with extra cookies was passed around as Ella reached down into a box and pulled out a few of the diaries.

She looked around the table and said, "I'm so thankful we were all able to gather today. I've read the notebooks and selected some excerpts to read. There's much more but I just chose a few."

Once everyone was settled she began to read what she had copied from the stories. She had chosen small sections that were in the stories but also were descriptions of real events in their family, substituting the family names for the fictional ones.

"Here's a short one," she said.

> *Going out to play Holly complained again that her blue*
> *wool mittens were too itchy. In Grandmother's*
> *dressing room, a pair of white cotton tea gloves were*
> *pulled out of a drawer.*
> *"Here. Put these on under the mittens and see if it helps."*

"Well," Cindy said, "That is certainly a memorable moment. It's becoming an endearing winter weather trait for Holly."

"And it works," Holly retorted.

"I had to include this one. I can still remember the chaos," Ella laughed and snorted, then added, "I'm not telling the one where I was laughing so hard and shot root beer out my nose."

> *After all the excitement and activity of Christmas day, it*
> *was well past 10 o'clock. I was sitting in the dark,*
> *thinking about the next day. Douglas, in his pajamas*
> *and oversized red socks, was trying to sneak down*
> *the stairs for a snack. He leaned back slightly to look*

*up the steps to see if anyone was up and, at that
moment, his feet slid out from under him and his
bottom bounced off the last five steps.*

There were a few chuckles and sympathetic comments.

"Oh, geez!" Douglas called out as he rolled his eyes heavenward. "Really, Grandma? That's in there? It hurt. At least I got ice cream on the way home."

Ella continued.

*He was quiet no more. Then everyone was up and,
although he insisted he was all right, there was much
commotion deciding who would stay home and who
would go to the emergency room and who and when
someone would call the other and which car wasn't
low on gas.*

Ella read a few more then said, "These are just a few samples."

She reached down into the box and brought out two hardback books and stood them up with the covers facing out.

"Now, here are books by Lucy Thompson," Ella continued. "In them I found the quotes like those I read in her books, and I thought Mom was typing up Lucy Thompson's handwritten manuscripts. I discovered that Mom was Lucy Thompson, her pen name."

Everyone's attention shifted to Ella. "Mom wrote these stories and more. The handwritten notebooks aren't diaries but are the beginnings of her stories. I don't know why, and guess we'll never know why, she kept this a secret."

No one spoke. Cynthia stood up, looking confused, and asked Ella. "How do you know that? Did she tell *you*?"

"She didn't tell me. I found files with letters, emails, and other documents in the cedar chest. It was business correspondence with her agent and people at the publishing house. I found out more and wanted to surprise everyone at the same time."

"Well, it certainly is a surprise," Cynthia replied.

It was a moment of realization in the group. They began asking questions, talking all at once, picking up and leafing through the notebooks with the blue lines of text and red marks. They were showing sections in the hardbacks to others and commenting that the author's bio states she lives on the Eastern Shore of Maryland and there are no photos.

When things calmed down a bit Ella spoke up. "I have one more thing to read and then we need to finish cleaning, make sure the fire is out, and then lock up. We'll meet up at Mr. King's office. But before we go I am going to share an email from the book publisher to Mom's agent."

"An agent?" Cindy asked. "How many books did she write?"

"Yes, she had an agent and over a period of fourteen years she wrote ten books. Here is the first offer of a contract in 1980. You might want to know that in subsequent books Ella Miller, Cynthia's sister, is featured in a series."

> *"The unique circumstances of the mystery and the twist*
> *in the story, The Purse, sets it apart from other*
> *mysteries. These first two chapters are well-written,*
> *and our in-house readers did not see a need for much*
> *editing. This puts this into the 1-2% category for*
> *publishing. Several of our readers suggested a series*
> *featuring Cynthia Miller would build readership for*
> *future sales. We are offering a $5,000 advance for*
> *two books with 5% royalties on this one. After two*
> *years of sales of the first book, we will negotiate a*
> *royalty rate for the second one, The Buried Box. It is*
> *also suggested that the published author's first name*
> *be Lucy, instead of Lucille, as it is friendly and*
> *casual. There will be other requirements such as*
> *availability for marketing included in the final*

contract. We will send it to Mr. Eric King, Attorney, with copies to you and Mrs. Moore." – Gregory Hawthorne

Later that day, at the reading of the Will, both Cindy and Ella were appointed as co-executors. Mr. King revealed that Mrs. Moore's estate had a large amount of assets, in the upper six-figure range, as a result of money from sales of her books in addition to investments, plus the house and property. Everyone was, once again, surprised including Mr. King who was amused to learn that Rose's literary career was a secret to her family.

It was decided that, as a group, they would discuss what to do with the money and the house. Since they were all together that day, Mr. King offered a conference room to meet. He also provided the names of a few financial estate planners who could help with redeeming investments, allocating distribution, trust funds and more.

Once they settled in the conference room, Karen and George said they would like to have, and move into, the house. Everyone readily agreed. As to what to do with the other assets they decided to give some to Alice Jackson, Rose's at-home caregiver for the last year. As to some sort of gift to honor Rose, ideas included planting a rose bush at the library flagpole, funding a writers' conference at Slippery Rock, and donating to the Icehouse Playhouse.

The sisters worked with an estate planner to review the assets and determine distribution to the family and what other projects were possible.

A few months later, Cindy and Ella met with the Director of the Lawrence County Library System. Collaborating with him, they set up a project to honor their mother. Funds were donated to the Wilmington Library to establish a local authors' area, Lucy's Corner. It would feature books by local authors and would include a small exhibit of Lucy Thompson's books.

And, in a small glass case, there would also be a few of Rosamond Moore's composition books open to pages of blue lines and red marks.

Author Bio

Carol Kagan is a seasoned wordsmith and herb enthusiast who navigated a 38-year journey to earn her BA degree. She is a devoted mom and wife, and the "crafty grandmother" of two. Now retired, she channels her creative energies into writing. She is the proud author of the book "Herb Sampler" in its second edition, available on Amazon.

DANCE PARTNER

by Sugar E. Cane

In the eighth grade, the boys' physical education class joined with our girls' class in the auditorium/gymnasium for a special program, social dancing. I loved it. If only we could have had dancing lessons in every physical education class. Dancing was much better than climbing those scratchy, brown ropes that hung from the ceiling or tumbling head over heels on the long blue mats. I suppose I do admit that some activities in regular physical education are memorable.

Shooting baskets was fun. I shot nine baskets in a row in a timed event. Then, for another exercise, we bent over in front of a wall, placed our knees on our elbows and pulled our legs up against the wall. Just think of a handstand against a wall. It really felt good to succeed. This many years since then, I think I can still do this. Or I like to believe I can....

The taste of different types of dancing won me over despite my successes in other physical exercises. The best part was when we paired up with the boys. Too bad it was such a short class for a short time.

To my surprise, I ended up with the cutest and most handsome boy in class. It was my great delight. His name was Jerome. It was not until now, as I write this, did the reason for my good fortune occur to me. The cutest and most handsome boy in the class did not choose me as his dance partner. This wishful dream misled me. The teacher put us together merely by pairing us alphabetically by surname!

Square dancing was fun. However, dancing face to face with the cutest and most handsome boy in class was better. As we practiced our steps moving right to left, stepping forward, then left to right and then back and starting all over again to the point of monotony, we talked about the upcoming school dance.

Two days later, in the early evening, the home phone rang. I answered the call and heard: "Hi, this is Jerome. Would you like to go to the dance with me?"

No hesitation came from me. He was the cutest and most handsome boy from the physical education dance class, asking ME to be his dance partner. Of course, I answered in the affirmative! How could I be SO lucky?

When we had physical education dance lessons, I continued to dance with Jerome. He was so cute and quiet, too quiet. As we swayed to the music, doing the box step we learned, I waited and waited for him to mention the phone call about the dance. I wondered if he forgot he asked me to go with him. What could I say to jog his memory? As the time for the dance neared, I finally brought up the subject in a general way: "Isn't it great we are learning how to dance for Friday's dance?"

A boy of few words, he was non-responsive. And that was that.

Now what? Such a puzzle. Was I going to the dance with him or not? Another day passed. We danced. We talked. Or I should say I talked. My partner was the cutest, most handsome boy in class, but not much of a talker or dancer.

Time is closing in to get an answer. Tomorrow, I will ask him outright, are we going to the dance on Friday?

Physical education ended for the day. I headed out to the hallway to my locker. I was confused. Oh, I am so glad I had not mentioned anything to my friends about the dance. I kept the secret about going with the cutest and most handsome boy in the class. I was too young to be embarrassed by being stood up!

Stopping at my locker to retrieve my books, I heard a familiar male voice call out to me. Here was my good friend Jerome who was in other extracurricular activities with me. He said, "Glad to catch up with you. Will pick you up at 7 o'clock and Mom's driving."

This chance encounter answered my questions. I mistook Jerome, my good friend for my cute and most handsome dance partner. I was happy to be going to the school dance. All this worry and uncertainty dismissed.

Lesson learned: Forever, make sure to know who is calling. Don't let a cute and handsome person deceive you into wishful dreaming. And, a good friend is someone to cherish.

Author's Note: My good friend Jerome, a wonderful dancer, and I won the dance contest!

Author Bio

Sugar E. Cane
Writer of poetry and prose. Inventor of useful household articles. Raconteur in local demand. Dabbles in acting.
Born to American missionary parents in Brazil. Named after the major export product of Brazil's economy....a story itself.
Greatest contribution to society: putting insomniacs to sleep by telling them never-ending stories.

WARNING: Refrain from asking the author questions unless you want to go to sleep. Should you nod off, do not be embarrassed, as this is a gift to you and humanity.

FRIDAY SECRETS

by M.J. Botelle

As old Matthew Sawyer gave a slow and steady tug on the handle of the heavy bank door, Mrs. Gleason rushed up from behind to relieve him of the weight. "Good morning, Mr. Sawyer," she said, holding the door while he passed through. "Isn't it a beautiful day?"

Matthew gave her a smile and a nod and made his way toward the line at the teller. Jim Scott paused in his rushing to let the ninety-three-year-old precede him. Matthew acknowledged Jimmy's kindness with another nod and shuffled up to the window.

Susan Kelleher beamed at him from behind the counter.

"What can we do for you today, Mr. Sawyer?"

"Just the usual, Susan. Deposit this and then make a cash withdrawal." His voice cracked a little as he tried it out for the first time that day.

"Same amount as usual?" asked Susan, eyeing the threadbare sweater he always wore.

"Yes, please."

Susan frowned and bit her lip as she viewed the modest figures in his passbook and deposited the Social Security check. By the time they took out for taxes, those monthly allotments weren't much. She counted his weekly $6.50, placed it in an envelope, and passed it to him with his passbook.

Matthew thanked her, his voice a little stronger with use. He slowly moved towards the door. Mr. Dunn saw him coming and hurried to hold it for him. "Good morning, Fred," said Matthew, "You're looking much cheerier than last week. Must be due to the good people in this town; always so kind and considerate."

"Yes, sir," said Fred. Things are looking good."

Matthew left the bank with a smile. Friday was the day he enjoyed most. After banking, he routinely took time to rest in the park before the walk home. There he could watch the town's next generation of children at play and see his friend, Teddy Benson. As he sat on his customary bench, Teddy's mongrel, Murph, came running over, followed by his young owner.

"Mornin', Mr. Sawyer. How's tricks?"

Matthew patted Murph's head and chuckled as Teddy scrambled up beside him.

"Pretty good," he replied. "How are things with you?"

"Not bad. This Monday's my birthday, ya know."

"I did. I believe you might have mentioned that before, once or twice. How old will you be again?"

"Gonna be seven," said Teddy. He sat up a little straighter and puffed out his chest. "Old enough fer school."

"That's right," said Matthew. "This year, isn't it? Pretty soon you'll be as old as me."

Teddy considered. "Well, old enough for a bike anyway. I asked mom for one, but she didn't say anything. I *am* old enough to ride one now, don't you think?"

"I do," said Matthew, "*if* you have your mother's permission and you're very careful." He had already had a talk with Teddy's widowed mother. She worked long hours at the mill. There was no bike money. From things Teddy had said, Matthew knew they barely made ends meet since Mr. Benson had been lost in the war.

"I tell you what," he said, "after I left you last Friday, I got to thinking. It seemed like I had an old Schwinn 3-speed some-where in the garage, just taking up space. Well, I dusted it off and gave it some oil and put air in the tires. It won't be new, but if your mother agrees, I think you might have it."

"Gee. That would be great! Do you think I could see it?"

"You ask your mother when she comes home from work today. If she says yes, you can pick it up tonight. You might want to paint it up a bit before the big day. I have found some paint for that, too."

"Great!" Then Teddy frowned. "She wouldn't want me to just take it, though. I'd have to earn it."

"Well," said Matthew. "If you want, my garden could use some weeding. You could do that and then the rest would be your birthday present."

"Deal," said Teddy, putting out his hand.

Matthew put his most serious expression on his wrinkled face, bowed, and firmly shook it. "Now, how about our ice cream?" He proffered a coin from his morning's banking.

Teddy took it, ran across the street, and soon returned with two cones and small dish of ice cream for Murph. The three sat in companionable silence, licking their sweet treats and catching drips melting in the August sun. With that fortification, Teddy went off to join a group of boys who were just organizing a base-ball game. Matthew ambled along the sidewalk to his home.

Mrs. Monahan was there finishing the wash. She shook her head in disapproval as he came up the walkway to the front door. She folded the last sheet and joined him in the kitchen. "Three miles, to and from the bank every Friday, is a lot for a man of your years, Mr. Sawyer, especially with that steep hill. Why don't you get a car?"

Matthew made no response.

"Can't afford it, I suppose," she grumbled, half to Matthew, half to herself. "Now, I've left a casserole in the refrigerator, should do you for two meals. When you want to eat, set the oven to 350 degrees and heat it up for about 40 minutes."

"Thank you," said Matthew. "I'm sure it will be delicious." He handed her an envelope with the weekly $2.25 in wages that he always paid right on time.

Mrs. Monahan made no move to take it. She looked at the simple furnishings around her and tried to wave it off, but Matthew tucked it firmly in her hand.

"How is life now that you own your home?" he asked.

"Well, it's a bit nerve-wracking to tell the truth," she said. "I thought, when the Taylors decided to sell, that we would have to move, too. Somethin' changed that Friday and by Monday, the bank give me a mortgage. It all happened fast as a summer storm. I asked how they could afford to let the house go for so low, but they just said it was their secret. So, I've budgeted that payment all in, like you said, but every month I worry that somethin' will happen. Might be there'll be another depression.

"I don't think you need to worry about that, Mrs. Monahan. Things are better now. You just keep to your budget and you'll get used to the payments. You'll see. And you'll pay it off in no time."

She smiled. "Well, I'd be glad of that and I'm glad I still live close by so I can squeeze you in twice a week around me other jobs . . . and make sure you have a few good meals anyway. Mrs. Sawyer would send a curse right down from heaven if I let you starve."

Matthew smiled as he watched her cross through the back yard and down the street towards home. She'd been cleaning for him nearly 10 years now, ever since his wife died, and she always hesitated to take her pay. His eyes misted a bit at the thought of her as he turned to follow her directions. He set the oven and placed the casserole in the oven before making his Friday afternoon phone call. That accomplished, he was ready for supper and a relaxing weekend.

On Monday afternoon, Teddy came by to weed. He was riding his new bike, which was now painted a bright red. "What do you think?' he asked.

"Pretty cool," said Matthew.

"Say, is that a new sweater?"

"It is," Matthew replied. "And what do you think? I just found it on my doorstep with a note saying, 'From a Friend'.

"Cool!" said Teddy. "I like the color, too. I'm gonna weed now, like we agreed, okay? N' I brought you the paper to read while I work."

"Thanks," said Matthew. He settled into a lawn chair and, for a few minutes, rested his eyes, Murph at his feet.

Teddy chattered on about this and that and in a bit, Matthew scanned through the news, the financial section, and the stock market, looking up from time to time to see Teddy's progress. He stiffened and sat up straight when he got to page 14 of local news. There were some pictures of an accident on Route 30.

> *"The brakes of a large truck failed as it sped through the light at the intersection and crashed into a car that was just crossing. Charles Kelleher, driver of the second vehicle was rushed to the hospital where he now rests in stable condition. Mr. Kelleher has multiple fractures and recovery will be slow..."*

Matthew rose to his feet. "Excuse me, Teddy. I just remembered, I have a phone call to make." He hurried into the house. When he returned, he was moving more slowly and Teddy was just finishing up.

"What do ya think?" he asked. "Does it look any better?"

"Oh, much," said Matthew. He forced a smile. "Now let me see how you ride that bike."

"I've been practicing," called Teddy. " Watch." He did some laps and turns and showed his stuff.

Matthew laughed and clapped. "Wonderful," he called.

"I have to go home now," said Teddy. "I have to help get ready for the party. Mom says she will pick you up at quarter of, and no excuses. It wouldn't be a party without you."

"I'll be ready," Matthew called as he waved goodbye.

He stood, gently rubbing his stomach. The moment Teddy was out of sight, he went into the house to search for Tums, his usual medication for an upset stomach. Then he changed his clothes for the party and sat down to rest, or maybe doze a little.

At a quarter to five, Mrs. Benson pulled into the drive. She got no answer as she knocked on the front door. She waited and then rang the bell. Still no answer. She saw no signs of activity through the windows as she went around to the back door. "Mr. Sawyer," she called through the screen. "It's Alice Benson. Are you ready?" Still getting no response, she opened the door and stepped inside. "Mr. Sawyer, it's Alice. Is everything alright?"

It wasn't.

> *"Matthew Sawyer died in his home on Monday night. The ninety-three-year-old sat to rest in his living room rocking chair and went peacefully to sleep. He leaves no surviving relatives. Born here in 1857. He has been a beloved member of the community these many years, serving on the Board of Education, as a volunteer fireman, in the Knights ..."*

The church was packed for Matthew's funeral. Ninety-three years of living in the same place had forged a lot of connections and it seemed like half the town turned out to remember 'Mr. Sawyer'. Stories and tributes, laughter and tears bade the old gentleman farewell with style.

As the crowd walked slowly away from the gravesite, Mrs. Monahan hung back and whispered to Mrs. Benson, "I hear it was you that found him."

"I did," said Mrs. Benson. "It was the second worst night of my life. I called 911 and tried to get myself together while I waited for someone to come. We were hosting six of Teddy's friends for a cookout, birthday celebration so I had to leave everything in the hands of the emergency workers, go home, and try to act naturally." She took out her own handkerchief and blew. "Do you know, he died with a present for Teddy in his lap? I didn't know what to do, but I took it home and told Teddy he wasn't feeling well, but had sent him the gift. Teddy was disappointed, but his birthday would have been ruined if he knew his friend had passed away on his birthday."

"I helped Mr. Sawyer wrap that gift." Mrs. Monahan dabbed her eyes with a soggy handkerchief. "He said every boy should have a horn for his bike."

"It was so kind of him to part with his son's bicycle," said Mrs. Benson. Teddy wanted one so, but we just couldn't afford it. I hated to refuse him. It was like a godsend."

"But Mrs. Benson," said Mrs. Monahan, "Mr. and Mrs. Sawyer had no children."

"Then, where did the bike come from?"

Three months later, Mrs. Benson arrived at the offices of Hayworth and Davis in response to the following:

Dear Alice Philomena Benson,

I am writing to inform you that you and your son Theodore William Benson have been named as beneficiaries in the last will of Matthew Walter Sawyer, who passed away on August 18, 1950. As the executor of the estate, it is my responsibility to ensure that you receive your intended inheritance in accordance with the terms of the will.
I have completed preliminary steps to settle the estate and am ready to distribute the assets as outlined in the will. You are invited to a reading of the same, to be held in my offices at 3112 Oakland Avenue, Franklin Corners, Pennsylvania on November 15, 1950.

*If you have any questions or concerns regarding your status as a benefi-
ciary or the estate settlement process, please do not hesitate to contact me.*

Sincerely,
Morton G. Hayworth
Executor of the Estate of Matthew Walter Sawyer

The office was already full and there were quite a few people she knew. Mr. & Mrs. Monahan, Mr. & Mrs. Kelleher from the bank, old Mr. Munson, Fred Dunn, Franny Kurtzwiler who worked the ice cream/soda fountain at the drug store, and Millicent Brown, principal of the elementary school, were all there. Mr. Hayworth, the lawyer, read the bequests. She gasped when she heard that Mr. Sawyer had provided a trust fund that would pay out a quarterly stipend for her and ensure that Teddy could get a college degree. He also left college tuition money for Franny Kurtzwiler and set aside money to pay Mrs. Monahan for housekeeping, twice a week, at Mr. Munson's. Money was being given to the elementary school for badly needed playground equipment and so on...

"Do you know," said Mrs. Monahan after the reading, "I received a notice last month, that my mortgage had been paid. I wonder..."

"Yes," said Susan Kelleher. "When Charlie had his accident, I thought we would never finish paying medical bills, but the hospital sent us a bill for just $40 and said that was it. I couldn't figure it out."

"And when my tractor broke down," added Fred Dunn, "it was like a miracle. George Miller told me someone had just abandoned a used one at the store. It was in very good condition and came with a note instructing him to tune it up, clean it up, and sell it to me for what that cost. I don't know what we would have done otherwise."

"I had no idea that he had any money," said Susan. "You

would never know it from his clothes or his lifestyle, or his bank account."

Mr. Hayworth interrupted the animated conversation and bade them all sit once more. "Mr. Sawyer was quite a wealthy gentleman, but he preferred to keep that a secret. He said he was afraid the knowledge might change how people treated him.- Most of his funds, in stocks and bonds, were managed by us. He made regular Friday calls to my office to check on his affairs and often gave instructions to help out neighbors in need, although he always made sure that they contributed a portion. He wanted to share his fortune, but said that too much of a gift, could take away people's pride or make them feel obligated in some way and they might not want to accept it. He thought a lot of all of you and said you all helped him in many other ways.

"I just have one last bequest that I hope you can help me with. I don't quite understand it. He has left a sum of money to the drug store to cover the cost of two Friday ice creams for someone named 'Murph'. There is no last name and no address."

Author Bio

M.J. Botelle spent most of her life in New England, where she taught French/Spanish in middle or high school. Mid-career, she began writing Christmastime, perk-up Seussical poems for colleagues. As family and friends had children, she expanded her field to include narrative poems and short stories written especially for them. She believes in All-Year-Christmas and loves travel, history, movies of the 30s & 40s, reading murder mysteries and music, music, music. She and her husband retired to Fayetteville, Pennsylvania next door to the State Forest. She now belongs to two writing groups, is experimenting with works of varied genres and lengths and is considering publication.

FAMILY SECRETS

by Roland Foster

This is a transcript of a recording presumably made by Mr. Alfred Pennyworth, who retired some years ago and left the city — it is not known for whom he intended it.

I have had a fascination with secrets all my life. I learned to read before age four, and that skill unlocked secrets for me that I thought were unknown to other children, some older than myself and already in primary school. Alas, I quickly learned that my "secret" ability was shared with many millions of others. Still, I loved to read, and I loved the idea of having secrets.

The comprehensive school I attended was unusual in that its library had been given a collection of American fiction that was deemed suitable for secondary students. In Year 6, in the school library, I chanced upon a Hardy Boys novel, *The Secret Panel*. What fun it would be, I thought, to disappear through a hidden panel into a secret passageway and pop out somewhere else in the house. I imagined that one day I might inherit or purchase an old mansion, and discover some secret passages — or create them during its renovation. It was a silly, wishful dream, of course.

In my teen years, I fell passionately in love. Roxanne was lovely, very like Mark Twain's description of Becky Thatcher — blue eyes and long blond hair, though without the braids. Should I confess to her that I adored her? Of course not! My love would remain my treasured secret, shared with no one.

Spencer Willis spoiled it, as of course Spencer would. He saw my gaze fixed upon her, and forthwith announced my secret passion to the entire world, much to the chagrin of both Roxanne and myself. I thought of killing him and hiding his body where it would never be found — that would be a whacking good secret, right enough. But murdering Spencer, while justified, was a bit extreme, and also quite impractical. Instead, I decided to discover an embarrassing secret of his and publish it far and wide. He, of all people, certainly would have guilty secrets.

Time passed. Roxanne moved away, Spencer left to go to Sandhurst, and I discovered Ian Fleming. Ah, to be a secret agent — what a lark that would be. "Bond ... Alfred Bond" — it hadn't quite the right ring to it, but I would adopt a better spy name when I needed it. Of course, I had no idea how to become a secret agent. But then, after giving it some thought, I realized I would prefer to have my excitement in rather smaller portions.

I tried university, but nothing that was on offer appealed to me. I dropped out before the end of the first year. Then for two years I worked at more than a dozen different jobs — waiter, bartender, lorry and limousine driver, packer in a biscuit factory, assistant cook, even cleaner. It was not that I could not hold a job; it was that none of those jobs could hold me.

I did, after all, become a government agent of a sort, but that is a tale I shan't go into. I tried it, I was adequate at it, but I found I did not like it. I bowed out quickly and fairly gracefully, promising not to tell what I knew, which was, in truth, very little. Then, almost in desperation, I left England and ventured off to find my future in the New World.

Newly arrived in a large American city, with little money and a British accent, what else was there to do but become an actor? Which, of course, I did. I loitered in places where would-be actors gathered, becoming one of many hundreds who were hoping to be "discovered." After only a fortnight, someone mentioned me to someone else who knew of a producer or director who was looking for "somebody British," and I found myself auditioning for a part in an off-Broadway play. Having, or not having, acting talent was beside the point; I was tall, reasonably decent-looking, and I talked a bit like Laurence Olivier. I got the part.

One evening, during the intermission, a man came to the dressing room I shared with several others. He gave me a card with just his name on it — Thomas Wayne. He asked if I would join him and his wife for a drink after the play. I asked why, and he said that he wanted to ask me something. Which sounded a bit off, somehow; and yet his demeanor was friendly, and he seemed eager for me to accept his invitation, so I did.

When I left the theater, Mr. Wayne met me at the stage door. We stepped around the corner to a waiting limousine, and he introduced me to his wife, Martha, and George, his chauffeur. We were swiftly whisked away and delivered to the door of a posh club, I think it may have been 21. The doorman knew Mr. and Mrs. Wayne, and the maître d' showed us immediately to a reserved table.

After a glass of claret and a few rather awkward attempts at polite conversation, Mr. Wayne came to the point. He said he had seen my acting, and judged I was no Olivier, to which I readily agreed. He also said he had had me investigated, locally and in London, and I was reported to be honest, a hard worker, and reasonably intelligent. Since his assistant was retiring, he needed to employ a new one, and he thought I might fill the bill.

"Doing what, exactly?" I asked.

He said, "I think the proper word is 'factotum' — in other words, doing whatever I need done. Part butler, sometime chauffer, occasional temporary cook — everything."

"Valet, as well?" I asked.

He replied, "Yes, sometimes, in a limited way. I don't need help getting dressed."

I liked the couple — they seemed genuine and sincere; and the idea of being a manservant of sorts did not put me off. It would be a pleasant change from my indifferent acting efforts. I mentioned salary, and he named a figure, which I mentally converted to pounds and found quite acceptable. Then he asked how soon I could leave the play and the room I was renting. "After tomorrow," I said, and we agreed that George would collect me the following day.

Thus began my association with the Wayne family, and it was a life far different to any I had ever expected to lead. Mr. and Mrs. Wayne were splendid employers, who treated me almost like a guest in their home, though of course I had many duties to perform. When I lacked a needed skill, I learned it, and fortunately I never tried Mr. Wayne's patience to the point of anger. What a wonderful man he was!

Their only child, Bruce, soon became very special to me. He was quite bright, and had amazing patience for one so young. He was five when I met him, and as he matured through his teen years and into manhood, despite the difference in our ages, we became fast friends. In public I called him "Master Bruce," and later "Mr. Wayne," but in private he was always simply "Bruce."

You may know about the senseless murder of Bruce's parents, right before his eyes. What is not generally known is that Thomas Wayne's sister, Clarice, then became Bruce's guardian. She moved into the manor, and I stayed on. After Bruce turned twenty-five and assumed control of Wayne Enterprises, he offered to "set me free," as he jokingly put it, with a generous pension, anywhere in the world I wanted to go. Of course, I had no desire to go, and I told him so.

That was when Bruce informed me of his plan to become a shadowy crime fighter. Naturally, I was apprehensive, but also quite enthralled, and not entirely surprised. We had talked of many things since his parents were killed, and I knew of his passion to oppose those who had no respect for law or decency.

We worked as a team to implement his plan, purchasing, devising, often even inventing what was needed; and I can say with some pride that I contributed significantly. We spent many happy hours together designing and building that splendid automobile. But my own most significant contribution, one that brought joy to my childhood heart, was the design and construction of the laboratory beneath Wayne manor, and the secret panels and passageways that gave access to it.

Thus, not yet in my dotage but well on the way to it, I found that my childhood dream of hidden panels and secret passages had become reality. And as the confidant and co-conspirator of the "Caped Crusader," I was privy to an astonishing array of secrets.

As young Dick Grayson, our Robin, might have exclaimed, "Holy wish fulfillment!"

Author Bio

Roland Foster went from graduate school at the University of Florida to five decades as a systems engineer, marketing support representative, and computer programmer — a career that morphed into publishing a monthly prison ministry newsletter, building websites, reading a lot, and writing about many things, amateur Christian theology being a favorite. He and his amazing wife of over sixty years live joyfully in south-central Pennsylvania.

SECRETS

by Jan Wolfe

I sat on the side of my bed, my feet dangling, watching the sparkles move. The sun was shining through my window and the sparkles were fascinating. When I moved my feet in circles, the sparkles moved in circles, and when I kicked forward, backward, forward, backward, the glittery sparkles flew forward and then back, forward, and then back. It was absolutely fas-cin-a-ting!

Something was trying to interrupt the flow of the sparkles. What was that? Something wasn't quite right; something was loud, annoying, trying to interfere... Focus on the sparkles; circles, kicking, sparkles, glitter; loud, annoying, interfering sounds. What was that? It sounded so familiar... I fell back on my bed, feet still dangling, and looked at my ceiling. It needed painting.

That sound! It's Johnny! I looked at the ceiling. Where was Johnny? I sat up and looked around. Where could Johnny be? I slid down onto the floor and crawled around looking for him. I stood up. I was a little unsteady, but was determined to follow that sound. Johnny Boy, where are you? There he was sitting in his car seat right by the front door. How long had he been sitting there?

"Johnny boy! It's okay!" I said as I sat down and got him out of his seat. "Let's change your very wet diaper." I carried him back to my room to change him and swayed just a little. I had just finished when my mom came home from work. She walked into my room with a big smile on her face.

"How's my little Johnny Boy?" she gushed. "Awww..." She kissed his little cheek and went to change her clothes.

I swayed a little bit and sat down. "Focus," I told myself.

Mom came out and told me something about plans for the day. I didn't quite get all of it, but mumbled, "Ok," to show her I was listening.

She picked Johnny up and took him with her to the kitchen. I knew she loved having him with her so I just sat there for a few minutes. I'm not sure how much time had passed but Mom was putting her coat on and as she picked up Johnny's car seat she said, "We're leaving for Aunt Laura's now. Do you want to go or do you have work to do?"

"Thanks, Mom, but I'll stay here so I can keep studying," I answered. I kissed Johnny's cheek and told him I loved him.

It was great to have some time alone. Nobody needed me. Knowing Mom and Aunt Laura, I probably had the rest of the day to myself. I took a hit and lay back down on my bed. The sun wasn't shining in my window now and shadows danced on the walls and ceiling.

"O-ver here. O-ver there. Now you're over here," my mind sang, to the tune of "Jingle Bells," as I watched the dance play out before me.

I fell asleep and dreamt of bells ringing and dancing and running into each other. Sun hit the side of a bell and I was blinded by the brightness. Then suddenly there were dark shadows and the bells turned black and fell to the ground, clanging and rolling and clanging and I was shaking and Mom was trying to ring one of the black bells but it wouldn't ring.

The bells were clanging now. They were so loud that they pounded inside my head. I wanted to hold my head but I couldn't reach it. How could my head be so far away? What was happening to me? Grasping... Where is my head? I can't even see it now! What is happening?

"Mom! Help me!" I yelled.

Then, everything went black.

———

My body shook violently, my bed was shaking. Something was in my nose. Something was in my throat! I couldn't move my hands. I fought and struggled and pulled; my body shaking violently, then I felt something cool flowing through me... my body shaking... feeling cold... then blackness overcame me again.

———

When I opened my eyes I saw Mom. Was I in a hospital? I felt jittery. Mom opened her eyes, and smiled when she saw me looking at her.

"Oh, Jamie!" she said and started to cry. She leaned down and hugged me and whispered, "I was so afraid I was going to lose you. I love you so much. Thank You, Jesus, for saving my sweet girl."

Still, there was something in my nose and something in my throat. "Mmmm," I tried to say, but I couldn't talk. This thing in my throat! I lifted my eyebrows to ask what was happening.

"Honey, you're going to be okay. You took a drug that was laced with fentanyl. Your heart stopped." A tear rolled down her cheek and her voice was cracking. "You were gone and the paramedics and doctors worked so hard to bring you back. Just when they thought it was impossible, you coughed." Mom's eyes held so much love. She looked at me and smiled through her tears. "It is truly a miracle you are here. Oh my dear, sweet girl." She buried her head into my side and just cried. When she finally lifted her head and wiped her tears, she said, "You've kept a lot of secrets."

I just laid there and looked at Mom. Her love for me so evident. Her concern so genuine.

"Honey, what a huge burden you carried. You don't need to live a life of secrets. You don't need to hide. You don't need to ever feel alone. I'm here. God is here. I love you and He loves you even more than I do!"

I continued to lay there trying to take everything in. I was shaking and my stomach felt very nervous. Mom knew I took a drug; obviously a bad one. Maybe she thought it was the first time? I needed the right words to find out what she knew. I avoided looking at her. What was she thinking? What did she know? She was showing me so much love and being so compassionate. She couldn't possibly know everything.

"Mom..." I tried to talk again, but couldn't and I started to cough and my eyes started to water and I couldn't breathe. My eyes got big as I tried to communicate with Mom that I was choking.

Mom's eyes got real big too and she ran to the door and yelled, "Nurse! She's..." And right as she was about to say 'choking', things started beeping; monitors were going off and suddenly everything was black again.

The next time I opened my eyes, I lay very still and looked around. I was in a hospital room and vaguely remembered seeing some of this room before. I wasn't shaking. I had an IV in my arm and a clamp on my finger; monitoring my heartbeat and I had oxygen in my nose. Whatever had been in my throat was gone. The monitors had a peaceful rhythm, with quiet beeps and a swishing sound. I felt strangely calm. I tried to lift myself up to get a better look around, but I was so weak it was impossible.

Mom opened the door and there was that love that I remembered seeing before. She closed the distance from the door to my bed very quickly and just hugged me and held me.

She whispered, "Thank You, Jesus, for saving my dear, sweet girl," and just continued to hold me. I admit it felt so good, so comforting.

She pulled back and looked directly into my eyes and asked, "Honey, how do you feel?"

"I think I feel okay," I whispered. "I can't lift myself up though. My arms feel so weak. I don't know what's wrong with me. Can you help me sit up a little?"

She looked for the controls for my bed and put the head of my bed up slightly. That was a little better. "My mouth is so dry. Can I have a sip of water?" I asked.

Mom said, "I'll go find out." She went to the door and said, "Excuse me. Can you bring some water in for Jamie? She's awake and asking for a drink."

A nurse came in right away, glanced at my monitor, smiled at me, and said, "Well hello there. It's so nice to see those beautiful eyes open. How are you feeling, Jamie? Any pain?"

"No," I whispered.

Another nurse walked in with a cup of ice water with a lid and straw. She smiled and set it down and walked back out. The first nurse said, "My name is Sarah. Here, I'll hold this for you. Take little sips; no gulping."

Oh that water felt so good going down my throat. Who would have thought one little sip could make such a difference? It felt like soothing medicine. I took a few more sips, then lay my head back down on my pillow. Oh, that felt so good.

Nurse Sarah looked at my monitor again and asked me how I felt. "I feel sore and weak; like I can't even use my arms or prop myself up."

"Well, that makes sense, Honey. You'll get stronger as you heal and move around. You are on the right road now and that's what's important," Nurse Sarah said.

The right road? I thought. *What is she talking about?*

Nurse Sarah fluffed my pillows, repositioned me, and gave one last glance at my monitors. Then she said, "I will leave you and your mom so you can talk. Press your call button if you need anything, sweetie." Then she slipped out of the room.

I looked over at Mom and there was that same look of love that I had seen earlier.

"Honey," Mom said. "Are you ready to talk?"

"What do you mean? Why am I here? Am I sick? Why am I so weak? What happened to me?" I asked so many questions Mom probably didn't know which one to answer first.

"Honey, it's time to let go of all the secrets you've been keeping," Mom said.

Panic wanted to consume me and take over my thoughts. What was she talking about? What did she know and how much did she know?

"What secrets, Mom? What are you talking about and where is Johnny?" I asked.

"Sweetie, Johnny is with Aunt Laura and he's fine; thriving really, but he needs his mommy and needs her to be healthy and clean," Mom said.

And there it was. She knew I'd been using. I avoided looking at her eyes.

"Mom, tell me what happened," I whispered.

Mom took a deep breath and her eyes filled with tears. "I found you lying on the floor, your eyes rolled back in your head. I called 911 and an ambulance came to get you. Johnny cried and screamed, hearing the sirens and seeing strange people in our house. I called Aunt Laura and she took him home with her. Those paramedics gave you Narcan and worked on you, trying to get you stable when you went into cardiac arrest. They worked and worked and shocked your heart and right when they were ready to declare you dead, Jesus made you cough. He healed you and held you through this whole past month."

Month? I thought! *I've been here a month? No wonder I was so weak!*

"They said you took a fentanyl-laced drug and it was meant to be deadly. They also said that was not the first time you took something. Your body was riddled with evidence of being an avid user," Mom said through her tears. "Oh honey, Johnny and I almost lost you. Jesus saved you."

This was a lot to take in. My first thought was that I missed a whole month of Johnny's life and I felt instant guilt. My second thought was that Mom knew I was a user and, weirdly, I felt very embarrassed.

My third thought was I almost died! That thought led to instant fear. Guilt, embarrassment, and fear; but my fourth thought was Mom loved me anyway. What the heck? Why wasn't she in my face? The love in her eyes made me cry. First one tear trickled down my cheek but then more and finally I just laid there and sobbed. In spite of all the stupid things I had done, in spite of all the wrong things I had done, in spite of the secrets I had kept; it was all out in the open, and I was alive and I was loved.

Finally, I took a shaky deep breath and said, "Mom, I am so sorry." Another tear leaked out of my eye. "When I was at Joanie's last year..." I took a shaky breath and did my best to continue. "I was feeling so depressed and she gave me a brownie and said, 'Here try this,' and I felt so calm. It started so innocently, so easily. It's way too easy to get weed or shrooms and just add it to your food, and because those are both more natural, I took them through my pregnancy. I thought it wouldn't hurt anything and I felt so good. I could get lost in the peace of things floating around me. I knew I needed to keep it a secret from you. I knew I shouldn't be doing it. I knew it was wrong, but I couldn't make myself stop. I felt so good at first that I thought if I just took more and took it more often that I would feel even better. But honestly, Mom, I only tried cocaine twice. Once with Joanie and once that day you left with Johnny. I just needed something to make me feel... better... And now... I just feel totally relieved that it's all over."

We were both quiet for a few minutes and then I said, "Mom, I just put you through a horrible, horrible month, and yet the love that I feel and see in your eyes is so moving. How is it possible that you love me at all? How is it possible that your love for me is stronger now than it was before?"

Again it was silent for a moment, while Mom smiled at me and a tear slid down her cheek. "Honey, the most amazing thing happened while you were lying here. A pastor from a church in town came to your door one day and asked if he could pray with me. I was so sad, so depressed, felt so hopeless that I said yes, thinking it certainly couldn't hurt anything. When he walked in and prayed for you with such compassion and asked Jesus to heal you, I asked Jesus to heal me. I told Him I was so sorry for all the times I failed Him and this loving, peaceful feeling washed over me and I think He filled me with so much love that you can see it in me. He healed you physically and I know if you just ask Him to forgive you and fill you with His love, He will."

"I want that, Mom. I want what you have. Will you help me?" I asked.

"Oh, Honey, of course I will." She reached out for my hands and as I lifted my hands to hers we connected in such a loving way, I was overwhelmed.

Mom said, "Jesus, You healed our sweet Jamie right when I thought I was losing her. Thank You for giving us another chance. Jamie, repeat this prayer. Jesus, I am so sorry."

I whispered, "Jesus, I am so sorry."

Mom continued, "I want to know You. Come. Fill me with Your Holy Spirit."

"I want to know You. Come. Fill me with Your Holy Spirit," I whispered.

"It's in Your Name we pray," Mom said.

I whispered, "It's in Your Name we pray."

And we both said, "Amen."

Author Bio

Jan Wolfe is the author of *'Twas the Time of Prayer*, a sweet story of faith, for ages seven to twelve. She is a retired elementary teacher and definitely has a second grade sense of humor but she does strive to have maturity in her walk with Jesus. Jan lives in Shippensburg, PA with her husband. They live within an hour's drive to all five of their children, all eight of their grandchildren and both of their great grandchildren! She loves spending time with Jesus and every single member of her family as often as possible. She loves to walk miles and miles each day and loves to read and write. Be watching for her second book, *'Twas the Time of the Miracle*. Out soon.

....

TANGLES

....

by Katherine Amt Hanna

Henry walked into the woods with a bottle of water and a heavy bottle of pills. Twenty-eight new Prozacs, twelve disused Paxils, and seven Percocets left over from a couple years ago. He'd added what was left in the bottles of acetaminophen and ibuprofen in the bathroom cabinet: several dozen each. It had to be enough.

There was no danger of anyone finding him before it was too late. Mid-morning on a weekday. Few cars in the park's gravel lot. His brother Jack wouldn't get the letter for a few days. Henry had the rest of the week off from work, so they wouldn't miss him until Monday.

He left the walking trail and pushed through the browning underbrush. Branches scraped at him. Thorns caught in his clothing, pulled at his hair. He didn't care. Almost over. Almost done. He used to come to these woods with Annie to enjoy the beauty of nature. Beauty had left his life.

He couldn't face another bleak winter alone.

Annie had always loved the snow, and had been cheered in her last month by several good snowfalls. He'd arranged her bed by the living room window so she could see out, watch the flakes blanketing the yard, watch the cardinals and finches at the feeder. But for Henry winter held memories of sterile waiting rooms and nights in the hospital. All of his loving care had been for nothing, and she had melted away like the snow.

Henry stumbled on. He tried not to think. Thinking led to despair, despondency. He'd made his decision and proceeded with his plan, so there was nothing left to think about. When he came into a small, relatively clear area he slung the daypack off his shoulder. He settled down with his back against a tree, cross-legged. A damp chill seeped through the seat of his jeans. He shook, and unzipped the pack, exposing the two bottles within.

Crunching in the underbrush off to his right. He froze, listening, watching. A faint wheezing and whining. Not a squirrel. It was coming toward him. He'd seen a deer or two in these woods, crossing the path well ahead of him, or across an open field, head up, ears forward, aware of him. They never approached.

A shocking mass of filthy fur pushed through the growth and into view. Henry couldn't tell what kind of animal the grayish mess of mats and brambles concealed. Natural dreadlocks gone bad. A hairball from hell. Bigger than a cat. Like some horribly ugly cashmere sweater knit by a blind, arthritic grandma and then dragged behind a truck for a week.

"Holy crap."

The thing continued to whine. It inched its way toward him. One little black eye glittered in the left side of what should be its face. Henry couldn't discern any legs.

He'd seen this sort of thing on the internet. Had to be a dog. Lost maybe, or discarded by some jerk, left to fend for itself in the woods of the park when it should have been coddled by kids, or maybe that grandma. Now transformed into something more pathetic and miserable than himself. Hard to believe what a lack of grooming could cause.

"How long have you been out here?"

A little pink tongue appeared below the eye, and the back end of the thing gyrated. It came right up to Henry's knee, a piece of it rising up, covering part of his leg. Overgrown black claws pressed against him through the denim, as if asking for help.

Can you spare a haircut, buddy?

A haircut seemed simple enough. But what if this surfeit of fleece concealed a deeper problem, a medical problem that required conscientious care? What if that care, no matter how tenderly or lovingly given, was in vain?

"No..." Henry gasped, and started to cry. He put a hand out, and the pink tongue touched his finger, hesitantly at first, then with more confidence. The whine became little barks and yips of joy. The whole hairy mass rolled, exposing four sets of claws, at roughly four corners. Henry touched the belly offered to him, tried to scratch through the mud-caked mess, while tears rolled down his face.

"I can't," he told the dog. "I can't. Someone else. Not me. I can't."

The dog didn't listen, just tried to rub as much of itself—himself, actually, Henry saw now—against Henry's thigh as he could, still squeaking and mewling.

A shelter tech with clippers could transform this into a cute little dog. Henry had seen before-and-after pictures, happy jumping pups released from the weight of their abandonment, the pounds of hair and mud and despair. Children laughing as the new member of the family licked their faces in thanks. A quick and easy fix.

Henry wanted that for himself, but after sixteen months of medications and therapists he had given up. "You'll be okay," Annie had said to him, so many times. He wasn't okay.

"Why me?" It had taken a long time to reach this abominable state. Why hadn't the pooch approached someone else?

The mutt made a noise, a gnarl low in his throat, that sounded like, "*Yoooooo.*"

Henry wiped his eyes on his sleeve and put his plans on hold.

He searched for a collar, a tag, but the mats around the dog's neck defeated him, and stank, too. The more Henry dug his fingers into the greasy, gritty fur, the stronger the stench became.

"You stink, you know that?"

More licks, wallowing, yelps of happiness. Fleas.

"Follow me."

Henry climbed to his feet, zipping the pack as he did, hiding the heavy bottles.

The furball followed him through the bushes and along the trail back toward the parking lot, squawking and panting. Henry wondered how he'd catch the dog if it wandered back into the woods. He wasn't wearing a belt for a leash, even. He needn't have worried.

His was the only car in the lot, now. He opened the passenger side door and lifted the dog onto the floor.

"Sorry, you're too dirty for my seats."

What did he care? He'd been about to abandon this car.

There was a vet just down the street from his usual grocery. The dog followed him in.

"I found this dog in the park," he told the receptionist.

She stood to peer over the counter at the disturbing creature by his feet. "Oh, my God. You should take it to the shelter if it's a stray."

"Can't you fix him up here?" The drive from the park put enough stink in his Camry.

"We could, but you'd have to pay for that. At the shelter you can just drop him off. Poor thing."

The poor thing sat himself down on Henry's foot possessively.

Henry pulled out his Visa card.

Author Bio

Katherine Amt Hanna lives just west of Chambersburg, PA. Her novel, Breakdown, is an atypical post-apocalyptic love story. Her novella, The Work of the Devil, has a sci-fi twist. Find them on Amazon, including in audio book form. She works from home making Medieval and Biblical costumes. Sewing leaves a lot of room in her head for percolating stories, but not enough time to write most of them down.

THE SECRET CAT

by Melinda Schwenk-Borrell

I was, as usual, running late for my appointment with my therapist. My mother had died the previous year, and I was struggling to make sense of a world without her. It was a cold January evening with the apartment's parking lot already shrouded in darkness. The visit to the therapist had to be cancelled, however. A cat was gripping my ankle.

I was fond of cats, but they had never been fond of me. When I was growing up, the family cat, Minou, would not sleep on my bed or climb on my lap while I was reading or studying. He was an in-door-out-door cat with an active life outside our home, where he patrolled the perimeter and severely chastised dogs who came onto our lawn. At that time, dogs were allowed to roam the neighborhood without their owners. So cats had to work diligently to keep the dogs from pooping on THEIR yard. Minou was very good at this task, but he also regularly got into fights with other outdoor cats who challenged him. His lack of affection for me was primarily fostered by my desire to dress him up in human clothes. After my sister outgrew her toddler shirts and shorts, I put them on Minou. Of course this was beyond anything a cat should tolerate, but my capacity to set limits on my behavior was still at a tenuous if not latent stage. I wanted

Minou to adore me but didn't know how to tempt or compel him to see me as snuggle-worthy.

The heartbreaking truth was that Minou was not ever going to be a cuddle cat for me.

But here I was, twenty years later, living on my own in an apartment in Chevy Chase, Maryland. On the way out to my car one frigid evening, a cat abruptly chose me to be its owner. She held onto my ankle with a determined four-paw clasp. I complied with this demand and immediately went shopping for cat supplies: food, bowls, litter and the litterbox. I resumed my counseling sessions the following week, but the real counseling was in my apartment with "Bootsie." Yes, I picked a silly name, but she did have two lovely pairs of white boots on her feet. The rest of her fur was striped from head to tail. I loved her in an instant, and she loved me back just as much.

Unfortunately, the apartment building did not permit cats or dogs, so Bootsie was my cherished and secret love. I couldn't help thinking about all the times society had refused people of different races to become friends or to marry. Now here I was -- a rebel, breaking down society's oppression towards having a cat in one's home. It was simply unthinkable that I would let her go back out to the urban wilderness of cars, buses, trucks, and dogs. She was mine to love, and our love was more important than prejudicial rules against pets!

My love, however, was tested. Bootsie was not a grown-up cat. She was probably nine months old and clearly did not know how to behave in a civilized manner. Her deficits as a pet were extreme. I didn't stop loving her.

First, she developed a fondness for going through the trash while I was at work, so the kitchen was covered with sticky papers, cans, and bottles when I came home. I cleaned it up and explained to her that dumpster diving was not proper behavior for a well-loved and sheltered cat. It took only three or four more such lectures from me for Bootsie to comprehend the message about trash remaining off the floor.

Her second pesky delight was to shred the shower curtain while I was away. This also occurred three or four more times before she realized it was an embarrassing practice for a dignified cat.

I loved the fact that Bootsie slept on my bed, snuggling close during the night. Minou had never done that before – I was filled with delight! However, before settling down for her rest, Bootsie enjoyed knocking things off my desk. I would be falling into a deep sleep when: CLUNK! The can holding pens was on the floor! I tried keeping Bootsie out of the bedroom so I could sleep, but she stayed outside the door crying. Cats do not ever like a closed door with a human in a room that they are forbidden to enter. It's their job to know what is going on. If you have ever had a cat, you know what happened when I tried to sleep by keeping Bootsie outside the bedroom. She cried. She scratched at the door. She cried and cried. And cried.

Yes, I let her in. After I lay down on the bed, she jumped on my chest and purred. I stroked her silky fur. We both fell asleep. A few hours later, CLUNK!

On the other hand, Bootsie always let me know that she loved me. She stayed by me while I ate dinner. She was on my lap when I read or relaxed. She liked play time, chasing after paper balls or catnip-laden stuffed mousies. She knew how to be with me when I felt sad or upset. My feelings didn't disgust or overwhelm her. She was just there, and there just isn't anything more comforting than having a cat purring on your chest, who then reaches out a paw to stroke your cheek. Reader: I had never before felt so loved or comforted.

Unfortunately, a few months later, as Spring returned and the sun's rays reached into the apartment, Bootsie's life as a secret love came to an end. Her preferred place when I was not in the apartment was on the windowsill, soaking up rays and keeping an eye on the birds. One Saturday, the lady who managed the apartment building came to see me. I wish I could say she was a horrible, mean, uncaring person. She wasn't that at all. She was kind and empathetic, but firm. Bootsie at the window had given us away, so I had to give up Bootsie or move.

I moved, and Bootsie went with me for the next fifteen years. I had been accepted into graduate school at the University of Maryland, so I moved to a house in Silver Spring, Maryland. That situation didn't feel right, so we moved to a better house with two other cat-owning women. The house was next to Sligo Creek below Dale Drive. This house was much better for us both, with plenty of natural wonders to enjoy outside the house. The creek fostered lots of wildlife, even though we lived inside the Beltway, just a couple of miles from Washington, D.C. A long-time birdwatcher, I was thrilled to see crowned night herons along the creek. A rufous-sided towhee family moved in and ate regularly at the birdfeeder I had set up in the backyard, even though they are not supposed to eat seeds. A mother opossum often strolled very slowly with her children along the backyard fence. Clever Bootsie knew not to attack any of the creatures I welcomed to our backyard. After her patrolling duties, Bootsie would join me in studying literature, rhetoric, linguistics, and the political power of language to subvert, subject, and distort. It was very nice to have a constant companion in these strenuous efforts. Nothing calms a fevered and confused mind better than a purring cat on your chest.

Much to my surprise, I received an offer to do more graduate work in Philadelphia. Would it be possible to take Bootsie so far away? Yes, the University of Pennsylvania has a veterinary program, so some of the local apartment buildings permitted animals! For five years, we lived in Philadelphia. Then we moved to South Jersey to live for three years. Then, we moved to Chambersburg, Pennsylvania. This last move was especially nice for Bootsie because she could finally go outside again.

By this time, however, she was no longer young. She had been on countless adventures with me, providing a constant source of warm affection. She had put up with the stress of six moves over the years, always adapting to the new environment, including several apartments where she could not go outside. Now she was in a home again -- and I bought her the best gift of all for a cat: a cat door! Oh, a cat does so enjoy having the freedom to come in and out as she likes! And, oh, does her owner appreciate not having to get up every three minutes to let the cat in and out as she likes! By this time, I had a year-old daughter who still was not interested in learning to walk. Bootsie and Elinor were gentle with each other and shared the floor nicely. We saw no tail pulled, no hissing or scratching. Elinor loved Bootsie's soft coat and appreciated having someone else who was about her size in the house.

By the time we landed in Chambersburg, however, Bootsie was an old lady. Her mischievous pranks were no more, but her loving warmth continued. It was tremendously sad to see her struggle, and veterinarians had no way to fix her ailing kidneys. I tried to give her saline drips below the skin to help her, but the procedure was much like a medieval torture for her. One day, a meter man saw me outside with an enfeebled Bootsie. She was skinny and walked haltingly through the shady part of our lawn. The meter man sternly chastised me for Bootsie's terrible appearance. He had no idea how much time and money I had spent in nursing her.

My glorious friend was grievously ill, and it was time to let her go. I prepared a comfortable box for her with blankets to give her warmth and comfort. As her time to die drew near, one of my other cats, a bruiser named Buddy, hopped into the box to stay with her and comfort her. He was with her when she died.

I sit here today with a cat at my side and a cat at my feet as I write this homage to my secret love, Bootsie. She sailed with me through calm and troubled seas. She was both stoic and sweet. She accompanied me through trials, ruptures, accomplishments, and the birth of my daughter. We loved each other for fifteen years – for 180 months – for over 5,000 days. Her memory lives on through a plaque in my garden: Bootsie: 1988 - 2003: Loving and Wise. Indeed.

Author Bio

Melinda M. Schwenk-Borrell, PhD, is a former professor teaching courses in communications, African American history, and rhetoric. She is now an online tutor for clients studying for standardized tests, writing legal briefs, and producing research papers for graduate school. She led the writing group at Coyle Free Library for over two years when she wrote some personal narratives, including the one in this collection. She loves books, social justice, cats, birds, French culture, nature walks, and her daughter, Elinor.

NAKED BY ANONYMOUS

by Kyle L Smith

I stood in front of the wall of my bedroom that was completely obscured by a grid of over one hundred cell phones. Carefully choosing one, I shut off the apps it was running and slid it into the pocket of my grey hooded sweatshirt. As I walked out of the dingy room, I tapped a frame containing an old, stained piece of cardboard three times for good luck. The worn and weathered sign had letters in black marker reading "Disabled Vet - Anything Helps" and shared its confines with a rumpled dollar bill and a handful of loose change.

You could barely walk through my apartment without falling over a work of art that had never seen the light of a gallery. Canvases stacked leaning against the wall had layers and layers of derivative paintings, while amateurish clay sculptures crowded the open spaces usually occupied by furniture. It took me five minutes to find my keys since they had disappeared into a meretricious wire sculpture that had taken over the galley kitchen.

I wouldn't be living here much longer, though. I was on the way to a meeting with the director of the city's outsider art museum. Getting a show in there meant you were in. It meant you were somebody mysterious, and everyone would want a piece of you. It was the difference between living a life of passion or slaving away in a corporate office until you were forgotten by history.

I don't even want to tell you what I had to do to get this meeting. Usually, getting access to these people is like trying to push through a boulder. Sometimes you have to be like water and flow around your obstacles instead of trying to grind straight through.

My roommate and his girlfriend sat closely on our lumpy futon, sharing a breakfast of leftover Lo Mein. I tried not to stare as I was still sore that she had been mine up until a few weeks ago. Sometimes the best revenge is success, but sometimes the best revenge is revenge.

Leaving without a word, I jogged quickly down the four flights of stairs to the street below.

———

I sat on the other side of a pretentious antique mahogany desk with a complimentary cup of espresso provided by the museum director's receptionist. Dr. Jilescue was running heavily late, and I was left to my own devices in her office while I waited.

Apparently, my time was worthless since I was nobody.

This nobody dribbled a thimbleful of hot coffee onto the desk and then set his coaster and cup on top to obscure it from view. This would be a permanent reminder that time was indeed a valuable thing. If it sat long enough to stain, then that was Dr. Jilescue's fault and not my own.

A half an hour later, the receptionist bustled in with the director while rattling off the tail end of what sounded like an itinerary for the rest of the day. It ended with, "And this is your nine o'clock, Mister…"

I rose and offered my hand, "Anonymous. Although, Mister Anonymous sounds better now that you mention it. It's a pleasure to finally meet you, Doctor."

The director was impeccably dressed in a grey tweed pantsuit contrasted by an ostentatious necklace that looked like a couture middle school rock collection. She eyed me up and down, obviously not impressed by my own generally rumpled appearance. "Have a seat, Mister Anonymous. I think our meeting is already halfway done, so you'd better get started with your proposal." She eased into her leather executive chair without a sound.

I remained standing and paced around the space, which I noted was roughly the size of my apartment. She got this much space all to herself just to have meetings, while I had to live in the same amount with a roommate who devoted his life to driving me insane. Well, that was about to change.

"I'll get right to the point, Doctor. My proposal is simple yet life-changing. I want you to give me The Atrium for four weeks for my exhibit. It will be like nothing you have ever seen."

She steepled her fingers, which ended in garishly manicured nails. "It better be if you want the whole atrium for a month. And what does your installation consist of?"

"Nothing."

"Excuse me?"

I stopped my pacing and spread my arms like a showman, "My installation is called, "Naked by Anonymous," and is true to its namesake."

"You want me to devote prime real estate in my museum to... emptiness? This is a joke."

I walked over and rested my hands on the desk. "Dead serious."

She rolled her eyes and checked the time on her phone. "Then obviously no. Don't waste my time."

I had her just where I wanted her. "Your board of trustees is pissed at you because your attendance and membership rates are down."

"That's absolutely none of your business and patently untrue. Where did you hear this?"

"Why do you care where I heard it if it's not true? You have officially bored the city to death, and without something wildly different, you will fade into obscurity and turn into yet another abandoned building that used to be something special."

She took a deep breath and leaned back. "Fine, I'm listening. But this better knock my pantyhose down and back up again."

I turned on my heel and worked the perimeter of the space. "Picture this, close The Atrium for two weeks with signs teasing an exhibit so controversial the creator won't even share their name. The whole time, you clear everything out of the space. No rugs, no plants, not even any electrical outlet covers. If you can remove it, it's gone. The space will be laid out completely nude, aroused, and panting with expectation."

"And why should I listen to you? I've never seen any of your other work. You're..." She gestured towards me.

"Nobody? I already told you that, Doctor. I may be nobody, but in the minds of your patrons, I'm the one who installed the statue of the mayor flashing the Financial District. I'm the guerrilla artist who painted the mural of children lining up to get bulletproof vests at the elementary school. If you play your cards right, then this nobody will be everyone in their minds. Since when have you hosted a titan such as I? Even Odysseus himself was once no man."

Dr. Jilescue swallowed hard, I could almost see the hook following the bait. "I'll have to talk to the board, but you convinced me at least not to throw you out of here. We have some time in early January that historically is difficult to fill, so it won't be much of a loss if you're wrong."

"It has to be next month or no deal. If you don't have the balls to go through with it, then I'll go across town to the Experimental Art Conservancy and let them bask in the glory. They might even be on time for our meeting."

"That's completely out of the question, we have the Atrium booked for the whole month with a promising new artist. They're getting ready to start shipping in the installation this week."

I reached into the pocket of my sweatshirt and pressed a

button on the side of my cell phone three times while maintaining eye contact. "Even better! That will only add to the intrigue if you shift gears and pull the rug out from under your patrons' feet. Can you imagine the rumors? They'll be crawling over each other to see Naked when it's finally laid bare."

"Well, you've certainly given us a lot to think about, but it seems we've run out of time. Thank you for your fascinating proposal, Mister Anonymous, but don't wait up for my call."

———

On my way out of the office, I walked past the receptionist's desk, took a seat in the waiting area, and checked my phone. The woman behind the desk looked at me quizzically. "Isn't your meeting over? Usually, people leave... Oh, if you're waiting for a ride, you'll have to go outside."

"Oh no, thank you, my meeting isn't over yet." I typed out a reply to a conversation and put my phone back in my pocket.

The young woman opened and closed her mouth a few times before the door to the director's office swung open.

Dr. Jilescue looked frazzled and confused. "Why didn't you mention that the board of trustees was already on your side? The chairman just texted me and explained the whole thing. I have no idea how, but congratulations. You're in. We'll do your crazy exhibition next month."

I slapped my knees and stood up briskly. "It's been a pleasure, thank you for your time."

"Jinnie, can you call the artist for next month's installation in The Atrium and cancel? Make something up, you're so good at that."

The rest of the exchange faded into black as I worked my way out to the city streets. The long walk back to the apartment was as delicious as the summer breeze.

———

I pushed into the apartment and chucked my keys into a dilettantish clay vessel that lived on an Amazon Prime box repurposed as an end table. My roommate was still on the futon, sans-girlfriend, but lying on his back with his arm over his eyes.

I looked down at him with a grin and playfully kicked his thigh. "Rough day?"

"You wouldn't believe it. I'm ruined."

"Oh yeah, what happened?"

He sat up slowly as I eased in next to him. "The Museum just called and canceled my show. That's a career-ender right there. No one's going to want me now when they hear about it. This was supposed to be my big break."

"Well, my roommate stole my girlfriend two weeks ago. Sometimes life sucks, buddy." I jumped up and headed to my room.

———

I returned my phone back to its place on the wall of devices and watched the bot as it kept chatting with Dr. Jilescue. It was amazing what AI could do these days. "Good job, little buddy, now get back to work separating fools from their money. Daddy's going house hunting."

Author Bio

Kyle L Smith is mostly humorous, sometimes serious, but always honest. When not spending time with his family, Kyle loves to create stories about pieces of his life blended with observations of the world around us. For links to all of his writing, go to www.kylelsmith.com.

POETRY

what god means by, "still green pastures and still waters"
or, ps. 23, or, the secrets of the climb, and sightings above stoned
gravel.

what of this psalm? this prelude to the climb, above stoned
gravel, to sight above,
around the ring, w/broken breathings rising in broken pentame-
tered feet, broken
meter, distant carews, w/salt wind, banshees keening, of pirates
& irish water

rising above the krill, the towers the stones; rising above, the
steeled claw cutting
deep, the cliffs edge, the sedge; rising above; the flash of orange
purple unsheared
woolen blaze; breaking the gap, the fence, tearing the stones;
voicings rattle to fall

into the wash of broken meter, silvered noise. the maidens dance to a silvered flute
in broken cadence, broken breathings rising in broken pentame-
tered feet; in broken
meter, mist-broken laughter, they dance with the waterville
ghost.

the climb above stoned gravel, to sight above, around the ring, broken breathings
rising in broken pentametered feet, broken meter; the climb into mist, the broken
stones, broken crypt; engraved stones, broken architraves, muckross' mossy grips

on bones covered, covers askew. the clutching yew, the abbey's covered cloister &
cromwell's sin; its silent din, fired limb, fired cassock, the smoky flow of tullamore
and ballyhoo, amber bubbles in leaded connemara lace; memory rising to dance.

the climb above stoned gravel, to sight above, around the ring, broken breathings
rising in broken pentametered feet in broken meter; the feral killorgan goat caught
in macgillycuddy's reeks, bleats; wynns folly, the troubles; the devil, broken tooth,

biting the mountain, spitting it onto the hillside above in cashel; satan's return with
his legions, slaughtered "tadhgs", in their 1000's, 6 deep on the cathedral floor;
blood & ash, stir the spirits, black murder in the air stirs rock, lane shadows.

the climb above stoned gravel, to sight above, around the stone's
broken breathings
rising in broken pentametered feet in broken meter; the rise
above holyhead stone;
the rise above the ulysses mv, & rolling roro, the lichen spattered
slate; st mary's,

the hollow, the white hazel, the whirlpool, the red cave, st tysilio;
to the slate sky of
preston; the luftwaffe grey above lady godiva's crypt; this
coventry yard, its
bacchanalian fest; light dancing in ash blackened shadows of st.
michaels spire.

what of this psalm? this prelude to skiddaw's misty heights,
would again be taking first steps upon aira force's
paths, rumbled wraths and rambled pools

from cascading fuel, falling from english stone,
calling echoes, ecco homo, from winding ground,
stumbled afoot, around, tumbled down, midland mains;

rotting manor's ruined walls, enclosed feld, stone exposed
haw, and ash thorn hedgerows, torn woolen tufts, bent
pipe posts, pipe gates, slick slate glazed encrusted,

blazed with lichens, with split-hoofed broken,
treacle glazed feld-stoned crazed lucerne, & birds foot trefoil
of florescent glazed hues, on the tails of singing ewes;

belly of ram, lamb, and worn shoe,
its stinging view, this disheveled tourist queue,
the dance of the traveling sisters.

***

herein within this midsummer's boxwood,
overgrown pastoral, steps, laid upon,

tramping on matted towpaths, footpaths plied
herein ullswater, within this albion wood

to, rumpled ways, limited breadthways,
its rubbled broken stays, splintered frays,

footfalls foregone, these bunyon steps, upon
this granite lith, lichened stoned, strathclyde.

these spattered bypaths, of this wayside, its
sheer glisten, the brush of its monkshood,

missteps, paled wan, its bane drawn upon,
into, this ragged deckle-edged foolscap.

india mattered isidro, misguide this
transposition, liana of the darkness

herein, entwined, vined, its goyan caprichan,
this midland pilgrims, disheartened umbrage.

befalls, upon, broken stone, upon, this
gangle, cloying strangle, through night's shade.

herein, linked in, inked in, ringed in, in
imposition, encircled arrayed chase.

enboughed, nocked, fletching embowed
wood's wraths, homeopathic polymaths

fleeting satin winged hydrophobics
in defilade before oz's gold cap.

here to......within this lures, emerald glade
within lurking shade, this circled brocade,

glint of, whispering silvered blade,
helio gravure, a fouled case arrayed

in a blake's oeuvre, the trees enfilade;
an ambuscade in shaded retrograde.

* * *

beyond the wall of hadrian, the barony, the climb above, its
embowed lure, its cure
for the witches; the birds attack within the shores of its virulent
nonesuch where
bobby turns to bronze, riddell to stone, and daffodils lie in
greyfriars kirkyard.

the climb above stoned gravel, to sight above, around steeled
rings, broken
breathings, rising in broken pentametered feet, the climb in
broken meter; this doric
monument to the dance of flames, bridges slide, its slide into
thames sludge.

beyond the wall of hadrian, beyond nessie's waters, maidens
dance at lomond.
beyond culloden, charlie & flora's flight to skye, the taste of the
mist of tomintoul;
three sisters stand in glencoe blood, watching the maidens dance
at clava cairns.

the climb above stoned unravel, to sight above, around steeled rings, broken
breathings, rising in broken pentameter, the climbs, broken metered, feet above in
wren's monument; beyond milton's stoop, the penserosa, the agonistus, the steps.

james p. barkley

BEYOND EL TORO OSBORNE

beyond el toro osborne
in sierra morena's
escalón de la meseta,

hidden
among glittering quartzite cliffs;
the dolls, the healing waters
the gardens, the sanctuary
among the paleo glyphs.

hidden
among the arid plateau's ledges,
beyond the blur of steeled rail
beyond the graveled berm
among the silvered edges;

pablo' remains in plated steel
along the A-4 south,
beyond toledo's landscape.

***

sierra morena's edge
steeled plate cutout braced in meseta sand,
still, alert, sentinel of the holy brotherhood.

spiny spanish broom, screes of broken slate
saffron and vine, olive and wine;
cervante's fete for hispania's tongue.

(seville, spain)

james p. barkley

ANCHISES' SHADOW

soil, black aromatic, fresh turned
spatters marble edging,
square, mars black walls.

what puzzle this, this space?
this pythagorean question, its suggestion;
these six faces cut into this elysian field?

what space this, does this theorem profess?
this area enclosing; depths of holy dark night,
absorbing soul and ethos, light?

this, rippled sine of linear sight,
oceanus' waves of cerulean bright?

these, shattered roman columns, at villa's west edge,
the heat burned thistle and sedge?

what space this, does this theorem address?
this, tower's polycratic, shadow;

this, domed iconic byzantine cross?
what space this? this stygian crypt, in sacred meadow?

***

for what virtuous hero,
or, heroic soul, does persephone call? do the zephyrs stir in
this plain's cicadian harmonics?

is this field, beyond the waves of the titan's crush
against the walls, against crusader stone;

is this field, beyond this plane on this blessed isle,
in this aegean strait;

is this field, for ajax to rest,
for kadmus, son of poseidon?

is this field, in my shadow,
for young aeneas in his didactic search?

(pythagorio, greece)

james p. barkley

THERE IS A MAGENTA PIETA

there is a magenta pieta in the matera car park above,
a blistered madonna, ragged poster nailed fast;
a la donna misericordia crèche in the ridola walkways.
her child is gone, its only purgatory that I see.
"how lovely is your dwelling place"

"christ stopped at eboli". and as the words would seem
the wheel of fortuna stopped, with st lucy's sightless eyes,
with enoch, the dark madonna and their latin cross;
stopped, at the blessed marble, gilded gold at the defile's
edge.
"even the sparrow has found a home"

he stopped before the rusticated skulls of del pergatoria,
with the sword of raphael to the left,
michael's to the right, guarding the rock's cleft
before the descent into flaking yellowed plaster passages,
"and the swallow a nest for yourself"

descending through the sassi gravina's division, uneven cobbles
descending, through massy calcarenitic tufo walls,

descent, to each his sassi portion from "la dolce vita";
the grate, sandled feet, torn knees, bloodied treads.
"blessed are those that dwell in your house"

detritus and treacle trickle down, down to caveoso cisterns
into fecal mattered manger scenes, vermin filled recesses
to the damned, banished, the massed father's flock;
to the damned, banished, the outcast mother's child.
"as they pass through the valley of baka"

———————————————————

a banished christ, no palms, no savior
a chosen barabbas, a vanished past descended
to barisona, caveoso's striken caste; found
the stones, the burro's bones, a socialist repast.
"they go from strength to strength"

a savior rose, another cast descended
arose again, to climb, from klegged depths
to matera's golgotha to hang and pass
into the heights; a saga recast, a cinematic repast.
"till each appears before god in zion"

there is a magenta pieta in the matera car park above,
the sassi gravina where her saviors descend
seek to view a last judgment, marble, and gild,
descend to b&b'd squalor, and disney'd pallor;
to rise from a vetted cast, with a tourist's repast.
"better is one day in your courts"

    (matera, italy ps.84)

james p. barkley

Author Bio

james p. barkley:
born into a "pleasantville" western pa valley,
into a religious community, full of music, church, family;
into an ethos of learning, work and travel, that still stirs and
burns
at the edges, sedges, the berms and sidewalks defining time's
calls and footfalls.
from his grandmother's knee, he has been drawn to the road, to
read, write, make art.
writing poetry has been the balance for his moving feet and
visual hand.
his education includes degrees in graphic design, photography,
art history and art education; this
followed with teaching high school art in north carolina and
maryland; working as a visual and
road artist, photojournalist, exhibiting in local, regional, solo and
group shows.
current chapbook: passaggii (compilation of road notes, jan.
2024) cyllarusrising@gmail.com

HEIRLOOMS

Sincerely thinking,
thoroughly discerning,
the person he was
to who he is becoming.
Raised to be compliant,
taught just to accept
detriment around him,
without inquisition.
His family never addressed
and pretended all was perfect,
assembled secrets, assigned disgrace,
so others would never notice
shrouds of deceit highly rooted,
cloaking flawless dysfunction
he now fights, struggling to
undo its undue traditions.
Crushing original cultures,
chipping molds which were
heirlooms from prior generations,
he's carving his own sculpture.
by Nancy E Reyes

LAUNCH

She sits alongside early events
that arrest the air in her freedom,
reviewing a strained isolation,
crowding her contentment.
Hoisting a torch to all she's covered,
exposing bits unintended for others,
clouds part as she glances up.
Sun smiles giving a gentle touch.
She is refreshed, reborn, refueled
as familiar stressors miss their cue.
Appearing to grow, spreading her wings,
she reaches, finding a morn within.
Beginning to move. Starting to breathe
without any discomfort to appease.

Looking at concerns she's always seen,
witnessing a launch of inner peace.
Recognizing wounds which happened then
are not a course in her present tense.
Embracing damage, letting it go,
escorting unknown, making it known,
liberation sets in, her essence is inflated.
She stands with her future reinstated.

by Nancy E Reyes

LODGER

Knowing all nobody knows.
Harboring what cannot be told.
Hidden. Darkened in a 4×4,
muffled beneath planks of camelthorn,
securing nothing's discovered,
permitting no one to uncover

> *true pictures...*
> *...ugly mixtures*

of your cosmetic design,
for an elusive disguise.
Crouching in stillness, ever on guard,
burying times untold, unsure of harm

> *from this invisible substance...*
> *...a massive obstruction*

overtaking personal existence
mapping roadblocked directions.
Led you where none could follow.
Built shame. Engulfing in its shadows

of suffocating blackness...
....a silenced abyss

that's alive in your being,
as natural as breathing.
Never questioning who, why or how,
when shown that which shouldn't be allowed.
"Don't tell anyone", was your precise order,
instructions to create a crypt in a corner

to lodge facts that couldn't be told...
....squash things not to be approached

stowing their actions beside deeds they did,
bartering yourself to keep it hid.
Ensured no persons were caught,
smiling, laughing to prove you forgot

acts they wouldn't admit...
...existed in an eclipse

ignoring the manner you were tossed,
like dirty laundry waiting to be washed.
But quietly pleading without telling a soul,
silently vowing, in private finding hope.
Wishing to be cleansed, peeling camouflage,
to release an awakening at dawn's beyond.
Exhaling, finally perceiving
how this burden impeded, came in between

every step, pulling...dragging...
...tripping, stalling, stumbling.

Intending to break out, to be freed,
ripping perpetual splinters among a scream.
Unload total mental weight with confined onus,
pardoning today's past brokenness.
You're ready to discard current beliefs,
anything classified, concealed. So much fatigue.
Back is sore, shoulders are aching
amid those skeletons you're sustaining.
Searching upward, extending eyes to the sky,
"Oh, Lord. Where do I start? Please, be my guide!"
A light cascades. It envelopes from above.
Warming comfort surrounds with trust.
You scan the air, welcome and safe.
A blanket rains as His words embrace,
"My child, drop each thought you are carrying.
Free your arms. Lose matters you are hauling.
For how can you raise both hands to pray
when they're heavily restrained?"
Tears well. Respiration slows.
Deeply inhaling. Palms unite in a fold.

Serenity...leeway...security...
valor...sunrise...purity...

New. Renewed. Lungs empty, fully relax.
Eyelids lower. All is detached
off darkness, affliction and sorrow.
Brightness touches, dimming its shadows.
No more gloom. Retiring guilt.
Understand concepts need rebuilt.
Prayers continue, asking for guidance,
feeling excitement, a blue horizon.

Bidding farewell to former rules,
abandoning, and agreeing to refuse
to harbor. Lugging it no longer.
It begins to end. Crumbling...under your power.

by Nancy E Reyes

HALLOWEEN

As ghost and ghouls
creep through the night,
a door creaks
revealing everything behind.
It opens with a moan
of Halloween's dead,
removing masks
off all we dread.
We tread inside
to face what's avoided
but divert our gaze
yon a hell that's hidden.
Stoned canvases
immerse our secrets
digging our graves
unless we confess them.
Mirrors are black
because our images are gray
over lives we've escaped
that we've given away.

We're weak with no hold,
yet at fault to a fault,
terrified to disclose,
visualizing our false.
But submerged further,
we realize a courage
too scared to stay quiet,
not disturb the disturbance
we've endured for years,
pressing us down
day after day,
intensely profound.
We listen to bravery,
a spirit of daring,
becoming our heroes
as we are reclaiming
those persons we were,
ending those we assumed,
igniting our glow,
reflecting only our truth.

by Nancy E Reyes

Author Bio

Nancy E Reyes began writing poetry in childhood. Her two books, "When Pain Smiles: Navigating the Rage of IED" and "Queen In Jeans: Getting Passed the Past", illustrated by her photography, relay her struggles with a mental disorder after a traumatic brain injury. Nancy describes her shame, awareness, acceptance, navigation and recovery since diagnosis. Contact: starpoems616@gmail.com

STOPPED BY SNAKEHEAD IN SEPTEMBER MIDDAY

Whose woods these are we locals know.
It does not sack and pillage though.
One open eye transfixes here
The awe at how pit vipers grow.

A little hoarse and cold and queer,
I stop above its path too near,
All its relations rise awake
The driest, hottest day this year.

It gives its flat black tail a shake
To taunt, "You don't see what's at stake."
It makes no tiny pebbles sweep.
This deadly calm no drink will slake.

For no sound reason, sensors sweep
As hands reach eggs in a hay heap
And infants stretch and toddlers leap
And parents mourn the price too steep.

Copperhead dreams are dark and deep.
They have no promises to keep,
No miles to go before they sleep,
No trials where fellow humans weep.

by Laura Mueller

WORM MOON, BLOOD MOON

Up at the hour of peak eclipse and stars,
A drop of light remained atop the orb,
And like a poultice drew upon my scars,
Their pain of loss and sorrows to absorb.
Recall a total lunar eclipse past
When I went out with Dad and telescope,
His range of friends a constellation vast,
My favorite part was when they'd tell us jokes.
Then further forward in my life, recall
Eclipsed up on a starstruck lover's deck.
His world with alcohol was in freefall.
He thanked me for that truth and my respect.
Too soon a shallow tempter sheds disguise.
The moon in shadow tempers a dad's eyes.

by Laura Mueller

SIMPLE PLEASURES

Breezes cool us from South Mountain,
Early morn and edge of evening.
Lavender and herbs abounding,
Caw the fish crow, quoth the raven.
Hummingbirds aloft and sipping,
Goldfinches on sunflowers gripping.
Fireflies rise up from their hiding,
Flash horizons with heat lightning.
Full-faced orange Buck Moon's eyeing
Shadow-rendered grounds smooth-shaven.
Gaia—goddess-god in balance—
Weaves from limbs an ornate valance.
Songs of praise for lucent guiding,
Grateful to be home abiding,
Solar lights glow all around us,
Color-wash our deck wood haven.
Bare toes grazing tender grasslings
Soon uncurl in dreams long-lasting.

by Laura Mueller

NOT OUR MOTHERS' SONNET

I hear you from an empty open place
Deliver biases you see in me,
And not one wave of sound disturbs the space
Or shivers the core of where we might be.
So solid is the ground under our feet,
No matter how much ground sets us apart.
So stolid what we found before we meet,
No chatter can confound the truth at Heart.
I hear you from this Empty Vessel call
And feel your drive embolden my response.
What importunity has cost is all.
No opportunity is lost, n'est ce pas?
Another rises when one branch falls down,
A hundred ways we kneel to kiss the ground.

by Laura Mueller

Author Bio

Laura Mueller retired from her award-winning private practice in the Baltimore/DC corridor to move north of the Mason-Dixon line. In American Acupuncture and Complementary Medicine for 30 years, she was also a researcher, publications writer, editor of faculty books, and post-graduate educator for Five-Element Acupuncture and Zero Balancing© nationally. Now her health research and articles at *TrialSiteNews* aim to help "Make America Healthy Again." Her fiction, literary nonfiction, poems and songs engage all five senses, emotions, and virtues for insights from observing Nature.

In Memoriam

Eric D. Bell
October 24, 1948 - July 23, 2025

Poet
Activist
Veteran
Missionary
Chaplin
Historian
Brother
Friend

HEAVEN DREAM

Authors write what ever they can imagine.

ONAJE poetry is NOT answers or fantasy...yea paths

My prescribing directive is...

Ephesians 4:29 King James Version

Let no corrupt communication proceed out your mouth but that, which is good to the use of edifying. That it may minister grace unto the hearers.

Eric Dennis Bell saved Christan, Chaplain and Historian American Legion Post 46. Chaplain and Historian District 22 Pennsylvania American Legion

Vice Chairman American Legion State Department Central Division Marketing, Media, Fundraising and Communication Division.

When talking about GOD, we are speaking from Holy inspiration from Christ Jesus.

Jesus the Christ, not secular, not ego, not man self serving.

It is more than good manners to give GOD the glory.

By Eric Bell

SECRET SLEEP

Sleep is unnatural time travels
artificial voyages seem unraveled .
Destinations removed and replaced
rearranging blending bending space.

Substance subtracted by imagination
left minded right-side blind invitations
leveraging new ways of seeing things
a dumpster diving a homeless offering.

Who put color come in darkness lighted?
Un necessary eyes and unfocused sight.
While you are driving without steering wheel
No guard rails, speed limits on how you feel.

A message without meanings at all
Full of holes in and back out you fall.
Full of wrongs that don't bother rights
And another one coming another night.

By Eric Bell

IF

Advents' shadow covering what's happening,
perhaps peradventure may be beginning thing;
see what a hidden futures unseen winds brings
Yin/Yang symbol balance in the flow of things
bring sense of shaping shifting mind pausing...
Yang aggressor Yin repressor yanks on causing
our blind conscience half-baked memory flung
at thoughts unfolding Yang before a Yin is done.
All an Advent anticipation action
About an unknown relation a flexible sum in an equation.
Time pulling of any IF
IF perched on a cliff...
to Step out look out
then meet with doubt.
IF seconds forever stop;
so, you must find out
on cliff deep as doubt
seeking it backed out
as one blinded by doubt,
dark as hidden heartbeats

letting IF steal earned treats or leap with faith rewards to meet.
(faith doesn't make things easy/it makes them possible)

By Eric Bell

WORD CASTLES

My poems are in each a word-built castle.
Eliminating all words that create hassle.
Welcome on to that ground floor
Exactly only the words I came for...
Ground up word concepts brew it
Sift and sew, your soul secrets to it!
When conceptional views can build from that
then at ground floor put out the welcome mat.
That right word in the wrong place isn't right.
Protruding their meanings reclaim their might,
Hanging them on the walls stick them to the door
reveal inflected connotation exposed at the core.
If a word won't fit, that word you must quit.
If a word won't roll then that word won't sit.
Don't marry words that just come quick
divorce your ego, from the first-time trick.
Translate easily forget the hieroglyphics!
These simplified rules can pick up the sticks.
Sticks of structure and mud for mending
being too smart will clog up the meaning!

Because:
Words are wandering arrows, like archers without their bows
First they flush the game; then their impotence they bestow!!!

By Eric Bell

Author Bio
Eric Bell
Premature 7 month in womb then I leave it.
Quickened conscious before physical completed.
White schooled raised, so everything could read it.
Sunday schooled son in segregated church believe it.
Scholarship won too late so drafted decided my life fate.
With that honorable discharge draft counseled my college living large.
Fortune from wars V"nam, Saudia, Bosnia Iraq as black man in charge.
Government inspector and contract management rejector,
Medal galore never wounded, yet PSTD in me regrets consumes it!!!
Onajeric, Onajempahty African American empathy

FANTASY + SCI-FI

ECHO STONE

By Brian Larrimore

At eighteen years old, Santiago had already told many lies. For his latest, he sat on his bed in the dormitory and pretended to study the spellbook. He had never studied, except for healing, so he probably would not get away with the lie. But he hoped he could at least avoid talking to anyone so that he would have time to prepare for the moment when Lilavati would return from the academy training grounds.

He felt warmth, hope, and anxiety when he thought of her. Warmth and hope because, although they had been friends for years, he longed for her and suspected she wanted him. Anxiety because a woman as beautiful as her had never wanted him. The way her golden eyes contrasted with her jet-black hair made him lose his bearings the first time he had seen her, three years ago, when they were sophomores. He had never understood how a woman's voice would make a difference to a man—until he had heard hers. She always sounded calming, in a natural way, unlike the rigid smoothness of someone trying to soothe a stranger. That night, she had cast fireworks spells in front of Castle Shoresky, and her robe and face lit with every color as she said the magic words.

Three years later, he still did not know what she saw in him.

He was muscular, lean, and almost seven feet tall, but his luck did not give him the striking features of the princes that ladies fawned over. His dark eyes looked sad, his eyebrows were too bushy, and his teeth, though not crooked enough that his parents were willing to buy potion for them, seemed goofy to him.

Beyond that, he had failed every class except for healing and was only permitted to graduate because of his exceptional skill there. He hoped to heal knights on the battlefield, or maybe villagers after a storm. But knights, not healers, ranked highest.

Santiago sighed with disgust that the knights, whether good or evil, seemed to have no sorrows, regrets, or fears. He did, and he knew that he could never reveal them. Before he had met Lilavati, he was recovering from losing his first love. They had been together for two years when she had discovered Santiago, in tears, attempting to learn healing spells to save his dying mother. She told him it was shameful for a man to cry and never spoke to him again.

He would not let Lilavati see that side of him. He would not risk never hearing her voice again. He would hide his pain now to practice hiding it for the time when he would become a full healer and see death every day. And he would keep hiding it.

He would have to make a hard choice. One of his classmates told him that Lilavati was going to ask him to perform the Echo Stone ceremony with her at Master Guo's funeral. If he did not agree, Lilavati would be hurt and angry with him. But, if he did, she would see him weep, and he knew she would be disgusted with him.

He calculated that, if he agreed to join her, he would only need to hold himself together during the first ten minutes of the funeral. Then, he could disappear. She would still be angry with him, but not as much.

He thought of how Master Guo had spent extra time every evening teaching him how to fight and explained how a fighter's mentality could make him a better magician.

"It's the same principle. You dig through a lot of practice and then

something happens without realizing it. It is similar to how you don't remember when you fall asleep. You won't remember when you become a master."

Santiago remembered how most students never saw that side of Master Guo. He was often disheveled, drunk, and gluttonous, even in the academy, one time accidentally setting a pile of ancient scrolls on fire. But he returned to reality when he trained with Santiago in the arena. Santiago's eyes welled. He doubted whether he could make it through the Stone ceremony.

———

Lilavati walked down the cobblestone path from the giant stone walls of the academy to the wattle-and-daub dormitory that stood next to the wheat fields.

She wondered if Santiago had found out about her secret. Chills covered her whenever she thought about what had happened years ago, when she had attended another academy. She could not think of anyone at Guo's academy who could have known, but, whenever a man she yearned for suddenly changed how he acted around her, she wondered if he had discovered the truth.

After it had happened, all her friends except for one had turned against her. The one had begged her to understand that it was not her fault. But if it was not, why did so many blame her? Could a whole academy be wrong?

She had chosen to learn how to make spells meant to pierce metal armor. She should have been more vigilant. If she had not heard of anyone else accidentally killing another spellcaster, would it not have been her fault?

After that, she swore to only cast spells for knowledge or for spectacle, such as fireworks, illusions, and manipulation of light for dining halls and royal chambers. She would not risk lives again.

She knew it would be impossible to redeem herself without

years of achievement in spellcasting, but she hoped Santiago would not learn about her past before she was at least close to redemption.

Stop thinking everything is about you. Maybe he does not understand how to handle Master Guo's death.

———

Santiago realized Lilavati had walked into the dormitory, and he jolted up. He stretched to pretend that his eyes were wet from yawning.

Lilavati glanced at the spellbook. "You don't even take the class anymore, you're pretending to study so you can get in an extra nap."

Santiago smiled sheepishly.

"I want you to lower Master's Echo Stone with me," said Lilavati.

"You want me to bury his secrets with you."

"Everybody's secrets are so personal. You were closer with him than anyone, I thought it should be you."

"And why you?"

"No one was doing it and I felt poorly."

"So many people talked behind Master Guo's back about how he drank too much and would break things, how he would eat too much and always be running to the outhouse. Funny, at least the first couple times. But I grew out of that and talked to him as a friend. He had a lot to say. Made me realize, maybe all of his immaturity stemmed from some kind of crisis he had. I don't know. I didn't ask, because we were friends. So he doesn't need me there."

"But....he's your friend."

A messenger shouted into the door of the dormitory, "Everyone gather! Someone stole Master Guo's Echo Stone!"

Santiago and Lilavati stared, wide-eyed, at each other, their mouths agape.

"How is that possible?" asked Santiago. "Only a very accomplished thief can steal an Echo Stone. Why would someone want Master Guo's?"

"Do you think he knew someone important?" asked Lilavati. "And they want that person's secrets?"

"Enough people mocked him in life," mourned Santiago. "Now someone's gonna share his most private moments with the whole world."

Santiago thought of the danger involved with chasing the Stone. The hunt would be Master Guo's way of training him one last time. If he could catch the Stone, he could be free of all his fear and become the type of man worthy of lowering it into the ground, hiding the Master's secrets forever.

Santiago and Lilavati nodded to each other, and they knew they would go together to bring back the Stone.

———

The brick and stone ruins of the four houses that had once ruled the kingdom rested beneath the dark green vines, rocks, and branches that covered their remains. The forest canopy grew thick a few steps, and water dropped from the heights to the wet leaves on the ground.

Lilavati thought of what it would be like if Santiago ever saw her Echo Stone and saw how she kept the spell accident a secret. Maybe saving Master Guo's Stone was the redemption she needed. She used a detect spell to find the faint outlines of footprints, and she and Santiago traced the possible thief's steps into the heart of the forest, where Castle Roots waited.

The wood of Castle Roots grew from the ground, first appearing as a tree trunk at the first level, then turning into lumber on the second, and then wooden walls with carvings that became more ornate with each level. A bird flew by the canopy, and the wood itself flowed up Castle Roots, each level of bark changing itself every ten minutes.

Lilavati and Santiago climbed through a door that appeared with a new level of bark, and they crept through shifting halls, the light coming from honey that dripped from the walls. A man with a silver hand and half a golden face walked down one of the halls, his monk's robe making him look like a shadow in the dim light. They froze, but he climbed the stairs without showing signs of noticing them.

They crept to the stairway and up the stairs to the second floor. Paper lanterns covered in glowing honey hung from the ceiling.

The golden-faced man leapt out behind them and swung a golden scimitar through the air. Lilavati fell backward and cast a protection spell, and the scimitar bounced back and landed on the floor. Lilavati and Santiago ran up the next flight of stairs to a room that looked like a dining hall with a few carved statues that changed shape with the new bark flowing up. They leapt behind the statues.

Growls and screams filled the air from the floor below.

The golden-faced man ran up the stairs, past them, and up the flight of stairs beyond, and then a silver light appeared in the upper flight.

A giant, white wolf ran up from the floor below, panting. Massive, bloody cuts covered her. "Can either of you heal?" she asked in a raspy voice.

"I can," said Santiago.

"That's too much for you," said Lilavati, "I need to—"

Santiago put one hand in the air and put the other one on the white wolf. He felt the wolf's body's memories of how it was before the golden-faced man cut it, and white fur covered the cuts again.

The wolf introduced herself as Sasha, rose to her feet, and growled. "Thank you, young man. The man who tried to kill you stole Master Guo's Echo Stone. His name is Carjetan, and he sacrifices people to monsters. Master Guo tried to stop him, and he asked for my help before he died."

"Do you have any weapons?" asked Santiago.

"He has someone upstairs," said Sasha. "He is drawing power from them. Free them, and I can break past the silver light and defeat anything Carjetan is creating."

"Don't we need weapons to cut their chains?" asked Santiago.

"I can break it with armor piercing spell," said Lilavati. "Just keep casting healing on me and yourself. And close your eyes when I give the word."

Sasha waited by the silver light, and Santiago and Lilavati ran up the stairs.

On the top floor, the bark rolled upwards into furniture, and the furniture changed shape. The branch thrones turned into different styles, and treasure chests and tables appeared and disappeared.

In front of the thrones, Carjetan waved his hands over a man with brown and silver hair, who woke up, screamed with terror, and thrashed in his chains. A shadow appeared that had the form of a giant bird with tentacles, and it crawled toward the man. Ten shadows in the form of knights appeared, turned their heads, and charged toward Santiago and Lilavati.

"NOW!" shouted Lilavati.

Santiago closed his eyes, and Lilavati cast a fireworks spell. She grabbed Santiago's hand and pulled him behind her, her trained eyes seeing through the brightness. She felt chills when she realized that shadow knights may not be blinded by her spell, but the knights stumbled. One sword chopped into her right arm, and Santiago's healing restored it. She found the man and, looking into his chains, pierced through them with her old spell.

The man fled, and the knights, Carjetan, and the shadow monster, adjusting to the light, charged toward Santiago and Lilavati. Santiago threw her on the ground beneath him and made himself a shield on top of her. Carjetan swung his scimitar toward him—and Sasha broke past the silver barrier, leapt into the Throne Room, growled and tackled Carjetan.

The shadows disappeared.

Carjetan, gasping his last breaths, looked up at the wolf.

"Die with my face staring at yours," said Sasha. "I'm the one who knows everything you've ever done."

Carjetan turned still. He unclenched his fist, and Master Guo's Echo Stone rolled out of a pouch in it and onto the floor.

Light shone out of it, and Santiago closed his eyes again.

GUO, AGE 29

Carjetan, in the dark academy hall, smiled at Guo. "Your proof didn't matter. We've already made it look like you were embezzling money. We can make it look like everything. You're finished."

"I'll start a new school. And I won't stop until I expose what happened to all those missing students and that missing master. How you've been sacrificing them all."

"Out to stop every injustice, are you? Going to stop hurricanes and earthquakes next? Injustice is like a storm. It's just part of the world."

"This is not the way the world always was. And not how it will always be."

GUO, AGE 34

Guo stood outside his academy, a single, small building. His unruly beard and hair covered a flabbier, older face, and stains covered his robes. A young, lean, dignified woman in scholar's robes stood with him.

"Why do you act like a drunk fool if you haven't even had a drop?"

"The Sunrise Hawks had their guard up after I tried to expose what they were doing. So to get them to relax, I'm pretending this broke me. That all I do is drink and gamble."

"I don't like seeing you this way."

"I need time to figure out how to find someone who can capture or kill Carjetan. He's the great sorcerer they all follow. When he's gone, I can stop this charade."

Santiago opened his eyes. Lilavati sat on the floor next to him.

Sasha had left, and she had taken Carjetan's body with her.

The flowing bark had covered any blood stains.

"Master Guo's dark secret is that he was an innocent man." Santiago's eyes welled up. "And even after he let them ruin him, he pretended to be worse than he was." Santiago could not hold back tears. He did not shake, but he held himself in steel stillness, and tears rolled down his clenched face.

After he finished, he realized Lilavati had been holding his hand in between hers.

"I don't want to give you any more burdens to bear," said Lilavati. "But I might lose the courage to say it, and I want to be honest with you. Five years ago, I accidentally killed someone spellcasting. Seeing what the Master did...makes me realize there's more to doing the right thing than hoping people don't hate you."

Santiago embraced her, and she cried.

He wiped her tears. "It was an accident. No one should have made you feel like that should have been a secret."

They held each other until the sun went down, and she cast a firework spell that created a small, dancing source of light to guide them home.

Author Bio

Brian Larrimore works in IT and writes science fiction and fantasy in his spare time.

THE WHISPERING VEIL

By S.E. Lower

In the Kingdom's heart of Solennia, jagged peaks loomed over shadowy forests that cradled Whispering Hollow. The village seemed to breathe with the land, its thatched roofs sagging under the weight of moss and its cobblestone streets whispering secrets with each footfall. At dusk, a peculiar mist rolled in, curling through the air like spectral fingers and carrying with it an uncanny hum that prickled the skin of those brave enough to linger outside. Village elders claimed the mist carried secrets—whispered truths and forgotten promises—to those who dared to listen.

Wynter lingered at the edge of the village as the mist rolled in, her fingers brushing against the ivy clinging to her cottage wall. She watched the tendrils swirl and dance. Her pulse quickened with an inexplicable yearning. She couldn't resist stepping closer, her breath misting in the air as she listened for the faint whispers calling her name.

She lived in an ivy-overgrown cottage, where she brewed potions and poultices for the villagers. Ten years ago, her mother had vanished into the mist, leaving behind only her journal filled with cryptic entries and warnings. She listened, hoping the mist would whisper the truth about her mother's disappearance.

Deep in her heart, Wynter knew her mother would never leave her. Someone or something took her away. She clutched the old, tattered journal, her fingers brushing over the cracked leather cover.

The faint scent of aged parchment rose as she flipped to the last page. The ink was faded, but the words seared into her mind resurfaced as she traced the lines: *"The Veil holds more than whispers; it holds the truth of who we are. Beware the shadows, my child, for they hunger."*

A shiver coursed through her as the weight of the warning settled in Wynter's chest, her grip tightening. She closed her eyes, hearing her mother's voice as if it whispered from the pages, urging her to understand the hidden danger and truth in the mist.

Wynter sat by her window, staring at the mist as it crept through the village, longing to unravel its mystery and find answers. The sound of hurried footsteps broke her reverie, and the door to her cottage burst open, revealing Kael. His dark hair was tousled; he breathed hard, as if he had sprinted the entire way. A faint sheen of sweat glistened on his brow, and his hazel eyes burned with urgency as he leaned against the doorframe, catching his breath.

"Wynter," he gasped, his voice tight with panic, "Mara's gone into the mist! The baker's been shouting for help, but no one will go after her."

Wynter froze, the weight of his words sinking in. "Mara?" she whispered, already reaching for her satchel. She stuffed it with herbs and a small vial of glow-essence—a potion that emitted light—her movements swift but deliberate.

"How long has she been gone?"

Kael shifted uneasily, running a hand through his hair.

"I don't know," he admitted, his voice cracking. "She was last seen near the edge of the forest. Wynter, we have to hurry."

The mist was thicker than usual, swirling like a living thing.

Villagers huddled near their homes, muttering prayers. All of them were afraid of the icy fog.

Wynter's resolve hardened. "Stay here," she said, striding toward the edge of the village square where the mist loomed thickest. "I'll find her."

Kael stepped in front of her, his hands raised as if to block her path. "Not a chance," he said, his jaw tightening. You're not going in there alone."

Wynter frowned. "I'm the only one with the best chance to find her."

"I didn't come here to send you into the mist. I'm going," he shot back, his tone leaving no room for argument. He hesitated, his gaze softening. "If I see her, I'll send her back to you."

"It's too dangerous. Nobody returns from the mist."

He glanced toward the mist, shifting his weight, torn between fear and action.

"I'm an outcast here. No one will miss me if I don't return." Wynter stepped closer, wrapping her arms around him in a tight hug.

"I need you to stay safe. You are my best friend!" she whispered as she pulled away. She subtly looped a thin, enchanted cord around his waist. He felt a sudden, gentle pressure holding him in place.

"Wynter, what are you doing?" he asked, trying to move but finding himself unable to break free.

"It's a binding spell. It will keep you safe until I return," she said firmly, stepping into the mist.

"Wynter! No!" Kael struggled against the invisible force.

Her heart pounding, she lengthened her stride to put more distance between them. *Keep him from coming into the mist*, she whispered silently. *Keep him safe.*

There was no one to listen to her, but she clutched her bag, ignoring his pleas, then his growls of frustration. She considered entering the mist many times before, and he talked her out of it. This time, the child trumped both their fears. She needed to keep the mist from claiming Mara as it had Wynter's mother.

The air clung to her skin, cold and heavy, like a damp shroud. Each breath carried a metallic tang, and a faint, rhythmic hum pulsed through the stillness, resonating deep in her chest as if the very mist itself had a heartbeat. The glow-essence illuminated her path, casting eerie shadows on the gnarled trees. Whispers tickled her ears, fragmented words coming from nowhere and everywhere.

"Truth... hidden... find..."

Wynter clutched her satchel tighter.

"Mara?" she called, her voice swallowed by the mist, but she pressed on.

After what felt like hours, she stumbled upon a clearing. At its center stood an ancient stone archway draped in vines and glowing faintly. Mara was there, standing before it, her small frame trembling.

"Mara!" Wynter rushed to her. "What are you doing here?"

Mara turned, her eyes wide and glassy. "The whispers..."

Wynter's breath caught. "What are you talking about?"

"Beyond the arch," Mara said, pointing. "A woman's voice. She calls for me."

Wynter's heart pounded. She glanced at the archway and then back at Mara. "We need to get you back to the village."

Mara shook her head. "We can't leave. Not without her."

The whispers grew louder, more insistent. Shadows coiled at the edge of the clearing, their forms shifting and unnatural. Wynter's mother's warning echoed in her mind: *"Beware the shadows, my child, for they hunger."*

"Stay close to me." Wynter uncorked another vial of glow-essence and poured it onto the ground. A circle of light flared around them, holding the shadows at bay—for now.

Taking a deep breath, Wynter stepped through the archway.

Mara clung to her side as they walked through the dark, shadow-filled landscape. A figure emerged, taking form from the shadows. A woman with Wynter's storm-gray eyes and hair streaked with silver materialized.

"Mother?" Wynter whispered.

The woman smiled sadly. "Wynter, my brave girl. You shouldn't have come."

Tears welled in Wynter's eyes. "I came to find you and save Mara," her voice broke. "I've missed you so much!"

"You've grown, Wynter. I might not have recognized you so grown up." Her mother's expression darkened. "The Veil demands a keeper. Someone to guard the secrets it holds."

"Why you? Why did you leave me?"

"You got too close, my child. When I stepped into the mist to keep you from going further, I became bound to the shadows."

Wynter shook her head. This was her fault. She remembered returning home to realize her mother wasn't behind her. This should have been her fate, not her mother's. "There has to be a way to free you. We can—"

Her mother raised her hand. "No, Wynter. The Veil's power is ancient and unyielding. Take Mara and go before the shadows claim you both."

The shadows slithered closer, their inky tendrils stretching and writhing like serpents. They hissed and crackled, the air growing colder with each inch they advanced, as if they fed on the very light and warmth around them. Wynter couldn't abandon her mother again. She reached into her satchel and pulled out the journal.

"I have your journal," she said, flipping to the last page. "You said the Veil holds who we are. This is not you, Mother. Please come home."

Her mother's gaze softened. "The Veil reveals our true selves, our deepest secrets. But it also demands sacrifice. To stay is to lose oneself."

A realization struck Wynter. "What if I take your place? If I become the keeper, you can be free."

Her mother's eyes widened in horror. "No! I won't allow it."

"It was always supposed to be me," Wynter said, her voice steady. "Mara and I can't leave unless someone stays. And I won't let you suffer because of me any longer."

The shadows surged forward, sensing her resolve. Wynter uncorked her final vial of glow-essence and poured it onto the ground. The light exploded, forcing the shadows back.

"Go!" Wynter urged her mother and Mara. "Now!"

Her mother's expression softened. "Please, Wynter, go. I can't hold off the shadows much longer."

Before Wynter could respond, a familiar voice echoed through the mist. "Wynter! Mara! Where are you?"

It was Kael. Wynter's heart thumped in her chest. How did he get free?

Her mother's eyes darkened with black rage. "Who dares intrude upon my domain?" She hissed, turning toward the direction of his call.

Kael emerged from the shadows.

"Stay back!" Wynter shouted, stepping back from her mother. Darkness swept over her skin and mist floated from her hair. Wynter grabbed Mara and pressed her behind her. The little girl whimpered and clung to her.

"You meddlesome fool!" her mother screamed, launching a dark tendril of mist at Kael. He dodged, but the mist coiled around him, dragging him toward Wynter's mother.

"Stop, Mother. Stop."

"It's not really her, Wynter," Kael said, struggling to get free.

Wynter blocked her mother's path. "You will not harm him! You remember Kael. He's our friend!" She cared for him deeply, more deeply than she wanted to admit. Nothing could happen to him. Not at her expense. Not like her mother. She swallowed hard against the fear clawing at her throat.

The Veil's power surged through her, mist rolling off her mother in streams. "Foolish girl," her mother sneered. "You should have gone when I gave you the chance."

Mara tugged desperately at Wynter's sleeve.

"Let Mara and Kael go."

"No one may leave the Veil without my permission. The mist is hungry, Wynter. It must feed."

The mist swirled around Kael. Darkness surrounded them. Wynter shook her head, tears in her eyes. With a fierce determination, she unleashed a burst of glow-essence, momentarily blinding her mother. "Go, now!" she urged Mara and Kael.

Mara ran to Kael, helping him to his feet. He resisted, wanting to stay, but Wynter shoved him in the direction they came. "Go!"

As Kael went to grab for her, the shadows yanked her back. Wynter turned to face her mother. "Please, Mother, don't do this."

The shadow figure closed in. Wynter froze. She drew upon the Veil's power, shocked when it came willingly. "You may have power here, but I have something stronger."

Her mother laughed, a cold and bitter sound. "And what is that?"

"Hope," Wynter replied, the light of the glow-essence flaring brighter around her. "And love."

The mist swirled around her. "I've never stopped loving you, Mother. I haven't ever given up hope of your return."

Her mother's form wavered, weakened by Wynter's words and the purity of the glow-essence. She found the recipe in one of her mother's books, grateful for its protection.

Suddenly, the shadow form slammed into her. Wynter gasped, her veins going cold. Her heart stopped for a second, or perhaps a minute, before it became steady once more. Around her, the glow-essence dimmed. The last of the mist cleared around her, leaving Wynter standing alone, feeling the Veil's energy settle within her.

"You belong to the Veil now, my daughter." In the darkness, she heard her mother's voice.

"Kael. Mara," she whispered, closing her eyes as she saw

them at the edge of the forest, safe and free. Kael turned back, looking toward where Wynter stood, a silent promise passing between them.

When she opened her eyes, she heard his deep voice declare, "If it's the last thing I do, I will free you."

Wynter watched them from afar. Her heart filled with hope, a bond formed in her chest like an invisible strand between them despite the distance. She turned to the darkness, a hand reached out to her. "You are the guardian, and I the keeper. Our duty is to protect those we love by guarding the darkness away from them."

Wynter took her mother's hand, glancing back over her shoulder. This was her purpose all along. A guardian. It gave her hope, and she knew one day Kael would return and she would stand between him and the darkness until her dying day.

Author Bio

S.E. Lower writes urban fantasy, paranormal romance, and epic fantasy, bringing readers into worlds filled with magic, hidden realms, and supernatural intrigue. Whether it's dragon shifters, fae, or the forces of darkness and destiny, my stories are packed with immersive adventure.

THE FUN HOUSE

by Laura L. Zimmerman

Violent shrieks of joy echo across the carnival Midway. The fragrance of popcorn and excitement saturates my senses. I close my eyes and immerse myself in the cacophony of thrilling rides and mouth-watering fried foods. The same carnival that has visited my town for all seventeen years I've been alive.

The ring toss vendor beckons me, oversized stuffed animals hanging from his tent. Lights that flash in every color of the rainbow travel alongside the roller coaster car as it rushes by, whipping wind and hair in my face. The *thump thump thump* of music blares from the Ferris wheel.

"Wanna do the fun house next?" Tilly straightens her tight miniskirt, then checks that her manicured nails haven't been tarnished.

"Sure. We haven't done that one yet." I rummage through my pocket and pull out my wad of tickets. "Huh." My brow cinches tighter than the belt I'm wearing. "I swear I had more than this earlier."

Tilly nibbles her lip-glossed bottom lip. "Yeah, I thought I did, too." She shrugs, her dark curls falling behind her shoulders. "Whatever. We still want to go though, right?"

"Of course. We've got to try every ride at least once!" I count out the tickets so they're ready in my hand.

A kid from our high school shouts something obnoxious to a few of his jock friends as he sprints past us as I shove the rest of my tickets deep into my jeans pocket. I refrain from rolling my eyes. Carnival week is a big draw for our whole town.

I follow my best friend as we weave through the mass of sweaty bodies and to the end of the fun house line. It's longer than any of the other rides, confirming that it must be better than anything else here. As we wait, I twirl my blonde ponytail around my finger, eyeing up the way the girl behind us drapes herself over her boyfriend like she's a ragdoll, carefully warding off any other girls who might look his way. They're a couple of years behind us. Freshmen are always so dramatic.

The large mirror that hangs just below bubble letters announces the attraction: *Freddie's Funhouse.* If I focus long enough, I can see the letters glitter, then change color. Tingles zip along my belly and down to my overly worn sneakers. Tilly and I have been waiting for the carnival to arrive in town for months. It's always the best part of fall.

A breeze brings a waft of fried goodness past me, and my stomach growls. Have we eaten since we arrived? I glance around, locating the funnel cake stand. That will be the first place I go as soon as we're finished this ride.

The line goes fast. Suddenly, I'm following Tilly's shiny black boots up the stairs, her fishnet stockings in my line of sight. As soon as we're in the door, our surroundings go pitch black.

I look down, unable to even see the band t-shirt I'm wearing. It's truly dark as night in this place. My fingers quickly grope for Tilly's upper arm, lacing tightly around it.

"Tilly?" I don't know why I whisper this.

In a flash, the lights go on and a clown pops from the wall, making both of us jump like a set of toddlers. I break into nervous laughter. The clown bounces in place with his arm pointing in the direction we should go. We stumble along, giggling as we enter the next room.

"Tilly!" I gasp, yanking her around a mirrored corner.

There are too many directions to go. She taps her long nails on one of the mirrors. With a devilish smile, she leans in and presses her ruby-red lips to the glass, leaving a kiss mark. She bursts into laughter.

I roll my eyes. She bravely leads the way, so I follow close behind. As we pass the mirror, I notice a few other smudges of lipstick where someone kissed the glass. Must be a popular mark to leave.

THIS WAY. A sign hangs at eye level, another arrow pointing right this time.

"Do we follow it?" I ask.

She huffs, glancing behind us. "Maybe? I mean, it could be a trick. To get us stuck longer inside."

"Does that mean we'll have to pay more?" I ask, my voice devoid of humor.

We run down the hall. A million reflections of ourselves flash as we pass. A streak of dark hair, a black mini skirt, and boots. The polar opposite, light hair and faded jeans.

Around another corner and then—

Tilly gasps. Her red lip gloss mark is on the mirror right in front of us. "We've gone in a circle." Her statement hangs in the air, bloated with disappointment.

"Boo." I grab her elbow, pulling her along. "Come on, let's try this way."

The path we take this time has fewer mirrors and darker corners. I internally yell at my knees to stop shaking as we turn each corner.

It's a fun house, not a haunted house. Why does my brain not believe me?

KNOCK. KNOCK. Another sign hangs at the end of the hall-way, this one on a mirrored door.

I glance at my friend, brows raised. "Awesome." My tone confirms this is anything *but* awesome.

Her broad smile tells me I'll have to face my fears and walk through the door. "Chicken?" she asks.

"The only thing I'm afraid of is clowns, thank you very much." I laugh as I pull the door open.

WHO'S THERE? This sign hangs sideways on the wall, which brings us to a dead end. We tilt our heads to read it.

"Oh," Tilly shouts with glee. She points behind us, then at the sign right in front of us. "It's a riddle!"

My mind wanders to those funnel cakes. "Okay." I drag the word out unnecessarily long.

We push around in the only direction we can go in tandem.

DON'T. This sign is low to the ground, right in front of a hole that indicates that we should crawl on our bellies to the next room.

"Don't?" I bite my lip. "Don't what?"

"Ummm, I think it's *Don't Who*, silly."

"Yeah, but what if it's *Don't crawl through that hole?*" I glare at my friend.

She rolls her eyes with a grin. We crawl through.

DON'T FORGET. This hangs on the wall directly in front of us once we've climbed through.

"Don't forget?" I whirl on her. "What aren't we supposed to forget?"

We finish our descent through another hallway. The two of us gather before the final sign of *Freddie's Funhouse* that indicates this is the end of the attraction, faces pinched in confusion.

Tilly sighs and flips her long hair, smoothing her skirt out as we walk through the exit. "Well, that was lame."

"I mean, I can't disagree. They should've been more creative if they wanted people to come back and do this thing more than once. I'm just happy it wasn't as scary as I thought it was going to be."

We step outside, the night air crisp and welcoming on our

skin. That same mixture of sugary desserts and fried carbs fills the atmosphere, along with shouts of terrified kids who ride the rollercoaster. I smile. Then a wave of vertigo sets me off balance. With a gasp, I reach out to steady myself. Tilly places a hand on the wall beside us, finding her balance, too.

"Whoa." She shakes her head. "That was weird."

"Yeah. It was." I blink and glance around. Something clings to the edge of my memory, like a dream I just can't hang on to after waking.

We walk down the ramp and stand beside the entrance to the game booths. *Click-clack, click-clack.* The roller coaster makes its ascent, shouts of laughter chasing me as the car rushes by. With each step that I take, a growing sense of unease snakes through my limbs. Like maybe I was supposed to do something that's escaped my mind.

The guy at the ring toss stand waves me over. Music blares from the speakers at the whirling and tilting ride. Giant stuffed animals hang above the rubber ducky game. The roller coaster passes by at an ungodly speed, a rush of wind and screams blowing across my body.

"Wanna do the Fun House next?" My best friend, Tilly, asks me.

"Sure. We haven't done that one yet." I dig deep into my jeans pocket for my tickets. "Huh. I swear I had more than this earlier."

Tilly taps her lip with a bright red painted fingernail. "Yeah, I thought I did, too." She shrugs. "Whatever. We still want to go though, right?"

"Of course. We've got to try every ride at least once!"

Author Bio

Laura L. Zimmerman has a heart for writing young adult fantasy with recurring themes of finding identity, belonging, and found family. She is currently a drinker-of-coffee by day, writer by night. Besides staying active with yoga, she's passionate about Jesus, singing loudly, and anything Harry Potter.

Her young adult fantasy retelling of Pride and Prejudice is releasing with Quill and Flame Publishing in 2027. She's the author of the award-winning YA fantasy *Banshee Song Series,* and two middle grade mysteries, all available with major online retailers.

Connect with her through Instagram and Facebook, or her website lauralzimmerman.org.

FINAL SECRET

by Carol Kagan

Take a brief moment and think of a secret that you're keeping from others.

You have secrets, I have secrets, and so does everyone else. It's something we humans do - hide stuff from other people. According to behavioral scientist Dr. Michael Slepian, on average, we keep as many as thirteen secrets at any given time. After research involving more than 50,000 people worldwide, the most common ones are lies we've told, ambitions, mental health, financial struggles, and hidden relationships.

What is a secret? Merriam-Webster lists it as "something kept hidden or unexplained." Slepian notes, "I define secrecy as the intention to hold back some piece of information from one or more people. The information itself is the secret."

But it's only a secret until you tell someone.

Is there a way to unburden yourself from carrying the weight of a secret without telling someone? Without revealing yourself in the telling? Without worrying about judgment or fear of the repercussions?

The answer is *yes*.

You can reveal your secret, anonymously, to *PostSecret*. This is an ongoing community mail art project, created by Frank

Warren in 2005, in which people mail their secrets anonymously on a regular or homemade postcard. Selected secrets are then posted on the PostSecret website or used for PostSecret's books or museum exhibits. (Disclaimer: They are only anonymous as long as you don't disclose information about yourself.)

It is easy to tell your secret this way. Take, or make, a postcard (more if you want to tell more secrets.) Tell your secret anonymously. Stamp and mail the postcard.

Tips: Be brief, write legibly in big bold letters, be creative. The postcard is your canvas!

Post Secret
28241 Crown Valley Pkwy #F224
Laguna Niguel, CA 92677
Visit Post Secret online: www.postsecret.com

ACKNOWLEDGMENTS

Thank you to Joan Pieffer and all of the staff at the Grove Family Library who helped make this anthology a reality.

Thank you to the writers and editors who are part of the Quill and Ink Society at the Grove Family Library for your creative ideas and talent! This project would not exist without you!

And thank you to the families of those involved in the creation of this project, for allowing us the time to write and work on our words.

If you enjoyed this book, please consider leaving a review on all major retailers, including Amazon, Barnes & Noble, and Goodreads. We would really appreciate it!

www.ingramcontent.com/pod-product-compliance
Lightning Source LLC
Chambersburg PA
CBHW030007010826
48973CB00009B/2710